About t.

Naomi is a simple girl who has always loved books and stories. They have made her a silent observer of life, of the world, of people. But they have also shaped her into a voracious, passionate, impatient and deeply honest human being, as the Brontës have. Their intensity and passion, imprisoned in corsets and good Victorian manners, their clear and, yet sometimes, unusual idea of what was right and what was wrong, echo her entire being. The Brontë sisters' novels and poems have been an immense source of inspiration for her poetry and prose.

One on the Moor

Naomi B.

One on the Moor

Vanguard Press

VANGUARD PAPERBACK

© Copyright 2025
Naomi B.

The right of Naomi B. to be identified as author of
this work has been asserted by her in accordance with the
Copyright, Designs and Patents Act 1988.

All Rights Reserved

No reproduction, copy or transmission of this publication
may be made without written permission.
No paragraph of this publication may be reproduced,
copied or transmitted save with the written permission of the publisher, or in
accordance with the provisions
of the Copyright Act 1956 (as amended).

Any person who commits any unauthorised act in relation to this publication
may be liable to criminal prosecution and civil claims for damages.

A CIP catalogue record for this title is available from the British Library.

ISBN 978-1-83794-513-9

This is a work of fiction. Names, characters, businesses, places, events and incidents are either the products of the author's imagination or used in a fictitious manner. Any resemblance to actual persons, living or dead, or actual events is purely coincidental.

Vanguard Press is an imprint of
Pegasus Elliot Mackenzie Publishers Ltd.
www.pegasuspublishers.com

First Published in 2025

Vanguard Press
Sheraton House Castle Park
Cambridge England

Printed & Bound in Great Britain

Dedication

I dedicate this work, "my Brontë narrative", as I call it, to the dear souls that cherished me throughout the winter 2022–2023 – the darkest period in my life – and to my close friend and second favourite poet (Emily Brontë being the first), Alexander Alexander, who had the generosity and patience to read it three times at least, make suggestions, comments and corrections. Thank you. My love for you all is volcanic and untamed, as were the Brontës.

Acknowledgements

Winter 2022 was dreadfully bitter on my part. The end of November had the taste of treason, physical violence and was tinted with the grey colour of the police station walls. Someone I had cared for, someone I had mistaken for my partner in life, hurt me in all the ways possible. My universe turned so dark and my prospects so thin, that the only means to find my way back to life, to the surface, was to reach for my loyal, immortal friends and mentors – the Brontë sisters.

I soon saw the likeness in our experiences – their alcoholic brother, my alcoholic former lover; a tormented yet loving relationship with their sibling, a tormented yet loving relationship with my ex-partner. And death. Grief. The end of November was also marked by loss – the suicide of someone I had loved so deeply and who had given my life the shape it still has now. My heart was draped in a black veil suddenly and a part of it will always be; my entire body was in pain.

I combined the Brontës' experience with mine and attempted to give intelligibility and clarity to what I could not yet understand and it took the form of a narrative. It was first a very short piece of prose I had written for a fellow writer and Brontë-adorer who was organising a writing contest on social media. I had read the rules, started writing, sent my work... and went back to it. I could not stop writing it. Each line, each word, was a balm on my skin and damaged heart. I remembered how much writing could be a cure and how the Brontës, ever since I was fifteen, had taught me to feel passionately, stay true to myself and to reason and have faith in hard work.

Although the words often flew from my pen, prose was mostly difficult for me. Yet my fascination for the Brontës and my need for an outlet made it infinitely easier. I had always wanted to write about the three sisters – my three guardian angels – and always needed to write about myself; I quickly decided my text would be a novel. A novel more efficient in my case than any therapy or medicine.

CHAPTER 1

The sky was turning pink. It was a light, smoky pink. Soft, splendid, promising. Slow, shy, yet resilient. It reminded her of a watercolour. It was a smooth tint to start the day with.

She could hear her sister's footsteps in the kitchen downstairs. They were light, too, but firm and hasty. Her sister knew her morning tasks by heart; they were always the same. She would wake up early, make bread with Tabby, take charge of the household chores and then disappear outside or in her bedroom.

Anne closed her Bible and allowed herself a few more minutes of peace. Her thoughts went far in the past, travelling from one memory to another before finding the one they were searching for and resting on it. They paused on a face she would never see again.

It had been nice to hope for a quiet happiness. To hope for a peaceful life filled with tender love and wisdom. Anne remembered his smell, its freshness. And his slow, still manners. And the way she would feel drawn to him. Even her father and sisters had acknowledged the good in him. He had charmed them all. Not a soul in the neighbourhood had not been moved by his natural warmth. He used to visit the poor, the weak, the sick. He had been a brightly lit candle in their obscure world. Anne had felt the lit candle in her chest, too.

Mr Weightman was kind, and God must simply have been impatient to have him by His side.

Anne sighed. She had to remember to be strong. She was in love with a dead man and it was no use to dwell on dreams. She stood up, put her Bible back in the drawer of her desk and walked to the stairs as quietly as possible. Branwell was still asleep, she assumed. His night had been agitated; she had heard him speaking and screaming in his sleep. She had also heard Emily whisper soothing words to him while carrying him to bed after she brought him back home from the pub. Drunk. Again.

Anne had helped her several times, but Branwell had pushed her away the night before and called her names. Emily said she would take care of him on her own from then on.

She went down the stairs and came into the kitchen. Her sister was putting the bread into the oven and Tabby was making tea. Emily looked tired. Her eyes were a bit swollen and she was thin. Anne was certain she had not got any sleep.

She asked where Charlotte was, for she had woken alone in her bed. In town, she was answered. Anne seized one of the cups Tabby had poured tea in and brought it to her father. The man did not like being interrupted in his studies; only Anne was quietly welcomed to help him with his morning beverage.

She gently knocked at the door and waited for his answer. He allowed her to come in. He looked busy and focused and did not pay much attention to her. His spectacles looked so small on his prominent nose and gave him such a solemn aspect. They made him look serious, as though he was always reading, always concentrated on some meticulous task that demanded to fold his eyes or have an ever-closer look at it. He looked like a man who did not want to be bothered.

Anne greeted her father in a whisper, put the hot cup on his desk, always in the same corner, and left.

Back in the kitchen, Emily asked her how their father was. He was well, as always. Anne drank her tea in silence. Flossy suddenly ran to her, greeted her good morning with her tongue out and her tail agitated. She was excited and impatient to go out. Keeper followed, stepping into the kitchen slowly with a pigeon in his mouth.

"Oh, Keeper—" Anne sighed.

She tried to seize the bird out of the dog's mouth, but he would not let her. Emily turned round and, without a word, firmly tapped his head. Keeper let go of the pigeon which fell on the kitchen floor. He looked up at Emily, hoping to be forgiven, but she was already focused on the cleaning of the kitchen.

Flossy hurried to the bird and approached her nose to it, curious. Anne pushed her away while Tabby took up the poor dead pigeon in a linen and went out to put it back outside where it belonged. Keeper would play with it later in the yard, or it would be stolen by some other animal or the wind.

The wind. Anne had a poem to complete and some drawings to continue, but she suddenly felt an urge to go out. It was still early. The moor would be chilly and unforgiving; yet she fetched her cloak and put it on. Ignoring her need for fresh and clean air was useless. Flossy followed her and enthusiastically ran to the door. Her tail was moving frantically. Anne laughed. The dog needed air even more than she did.

Anne warned her sister she was going for a walk and left the house. She knew the shortest way to the moor; so did Flossy. Together, they followed the path they had known forever.

Anne had been right. The wind was cold but pure. Spring and summer warmths were soothing but did not have the honesty that autumn and winter breaths offered. The cold suited her soul. And it was the end of autumn, that period in the year during which the weather and the hills seemed to hesitate between different temperatures, between various shades of colours. Even nature could be indecisive. Anne found it comforting.

Flossy was running wild, her ears jumping up and down. She was breathing in the wind, chasing butterflies. Anne smiled.

She arrived at the lonely parts of the moor, where she rarely met a human soul. She closed her eyes and the wind seemed to whisper a line or two to her. She regretted that she had not brought her pencil and notebook; she would have to memorise them.

When she opened her eyes again, the colours looked so bright to her. Some bushes were timid green, others openly purple. There was no limit above, no frontier between the hills and the sky. Which was no longer pink but slowly turning grey. A gigantic cloud was approaching, as though trying to gently stroke it. It had a strange hue, perhaps, because it was made of several. Anne could see dark blue, pink again and light grey. She was standing inside a painting.

She kept going a little further, unwilling to feel locked in again. She cherished the parsonage, the peace and quiet she could sometimes find in it and loved the souls who peopled it. But the wind was sometimes a song to her ears, a song that would call out her name. She could never resist it. She had missed it when she had been away and she had been away for so long. It had felt like she had abandoned a piece of herself in the moors, a piece she had not been able to replace in Mirfield or York.

But now she was back. For good.

Flossy barked at her, desperate to get her attention. Anne looked up. The colour of the cloud was slightly changed; it now reminded her of Emily's eyes.

She answered Flossy and pulled her skirts a little up to ease her way nearer to her. The dog had caught a crow. She dropped it at Anne's feet, expecting a reward. Anne sighed and stroked her behind the ears. She did not like it when her pet killed other animals but was incapable of scolding her the way her sister did with her own dog.

They left the crow to the moor, like a gift to the wild, and kept walking, penetrating the painting even deeper. The horizon was endless; perhaps they had been there for hours, perhaps days. One could never tell. Time made no sense there. The moors had their own laws and followed no human schedule.

Anne had to slow her pace. Her corset was making her breathing difficult and the weight of her dress made her sweat. In her slowed movements and breath, she found a pace she would later use in a poem. The moor had offered her its usual present: she felt inspired – they would have to go back soon.

Their way back to the house was quick. Flossy looked disappointed, but Anne was unyielding. She had to write.

They arrived at the parsonage. Anne went into the dining room and warmed her hands by the fire before going straight upstairs to the bedroom she shared with Charlotte. She took her notebook, ink and steel pen and went back down to the dining room, where she immediately wrote down the lines she had in mind.

After a few minutes, she dropped her pen and breathed out. It was as though she had not relaxed since the lines had entered her head.

There they were. Written down. Safe. They could not get lost in her brain or be forgotten in some dark place of her memory.

She read them again and then started making some corrections. She would need Emily to read them, too. She often required her opinion. Anne knew she should have been more confident about her work, yet poetry was pitiless. The story she had completed a few months ago had felt more natural to weave. It had long remained a humming project in her head, a draft, and Anne, at first, had not known where it would lead exactly, yet she had not been able to stop writing it. Every time she worked on it, she felt something in her stomach loosen up, for her experiences as a governess had not always been easy and pleasant. Living away from her family and her favourite landscapes had been nearly traumatic. She had forced herself to keep going and not to ever complain, but a mass had formed in her body – a mass of frustration and words. She had had to release it.

She wondered if the last publishers her sisters and she had sent their works to would see what she felt during that period of time. What they three could feel, see, hear, imagine. Who they were. Would they guess they were women? Would they decide it was improper for women to write? To write stories as intense as theirs? Could it matter whether the writers were men or women? She was satisfied with a good book whatever the sex of the author might have been.[1] Would the publishers feel the same? And if they did, would they enjoy their reading? Would they read their works at all or simply send them back, judging them worthless because they saw them as being written by some obscure nobodies?

Sometimes, when the world around her felt on the verge of collapsing, Anne would cling to her hope of having made something – a book. A story that would transcend space and time. The poems that her sisters and she had managed to get published had been a financial failure, yet Anne did not despair and though her faith in their talents was quiet, it was also fierce.

---

[1] Preface by Anne Brontë to the second edition *The Tenant of Wildfell Hall*

Anne's pulse was quick. She had to calm down. She closed her eyes and eased her breathing. It was noon when she opened them again and read her work for the tenth time.

Suddenly, she heard a noise from upstairs. Branwell was getting up, probably suffering from what he would call a brain fever and lurching as something fell down and resonated in the dining room. Anne briskly closed her notebook – her brother did not know the three of them wrote – and gathered her things, ready to rush back up to her room and hide them there.

But Branwell was going down the stairs. She could hear his unsure steps and he barged into the dining room which looked so narrow suddenly. The daylight crossing the windowpane made the look in his eyes even wilder. They were dark, his eyes, and damp – wet with the drinks of the previous night.

Anne looked down. It was painful to see her brother lose control of himself so vehemently. Why could he not try, at least? Why had he given in so easily? They all had lost companions who had been dear to their hearts; why was he the only one who was allowed to show it? And show it repeatedly.

"Morning, Anne."

"It's noon."

Branwell staggered to the closest chair and heavily sat down, his body an immense burden. He sighed. Anne could smell his thick, foul breath from where she was standing. It was a hot, dizzying smell made of bitter beer, whisky and lack of hygiene. It reminded her of the day he was so drunk that he vomited on his shirt and she had to wash him. Wash her own adult brother.

She looked away.

He looked calm now, however, gazing at the yard through the window; so, she silently walked to the door, trying to escape. When she got near him, he caught her arm and told her he did not remember what he had done or said the night before. Anne did not reply; there was nothing to say. Every day, her brother would claim he had no recollection of his wrong deeds or hurtful words. None of his sisters believed him. Right and wrong did not exist in a drunk's mind. Truth and lies were indistinct.

Anne freed her arm and left the room. Upstairs, she left her things in her drawers and went back down to the kitchen to help her sister and Tabby with the daily chores. Cleaning, dusting and washing would help clear her mind, no doubt.

The two women asked her if Branwell was awake. They must have heard him. She said he was.

Anne helped with the cooking and the sweeping. She hung up the laundry and helped Tabby set the table in the dining room. Branwell was standing at the fireplace now, contemplating the flames. He mumbled something and Anne thought she recognised a poem by Byron. But she ignored him. She walked to the hall and knocked at the door of her father's study again. She told him lunch was ready. She always called him to meals before the food was actually on the table, for she knew her father would first finish whatever work he was doing before joining them in the dining room.

Anne took a seat at the dining table. She was hungry. She looked at Emily, who was whispering to Branwell, his hand in hers, probably trying to convince him to have some food. She looked at Charlotte, who had got back from errands and was helping Tabby fill the plates. She looked at her brother, who was clearly torturing their sister and expecting more pleading from her. And she thought of her father, who had spent the entire morning in the quiet of his study, surrounded by books and not expected in the kitchen or anywhere else in the parsonage.

Emily was too patient with Branwell. He was the only person she was so forgiving with, for she knew he was weak. She would have been patient with her too, perhaps. Yes, surely. But Anne had never had to challenge her sister's indulgence.

Charlotte simply ignored him. She would sometimes look close to him, but her eyes would never stop on his actual figure. Anne knew Charlotte was hurt; she knew she would never understand such surrender. They had both undergone the same passion, obsession, the same wrecking mental torture; yet she had made an utterly different decision. She had chosen to flee, run away from sin. He had allowed it to invade him, had lingered in it, drowned in it, relished its bitter taste. Anne understood Charlotte's disapproval, but she also suspected her sister envied their brother's capacity to give in. She would never allow herself such infamy – such freedom. Anne praised her sister's integrity and despised Branwell's immorality but wondered how two siblings who had been so close could have become such different individuals.

They started lunch in silence. The soup was thick and nourishing, the bread Emily had made was tasty and light as the air. Their father not once looked up to them, but asked Charlotte if the town was busy. Charlotte answered it was not. People preferred to go out in the afternoon because the air was so fresh at the time she had left. Their father said fresh air was good for one's lungs. Charlotte did not answer. Anne knew her sister had gone out to send their works to another publisher in London and asked her father what he was studying. He was reading psalms again to prepare Sunday's sermon. Anne asked if he had found anything new in them. He said there was always something new to find in them.

Branwell abruptly got up, startling his family and spilling water on the table and left the room. Anne turned round to see where he was going and saw him seize his cloak. They heard him open and then slam the door. Emily was staring at their father in her unperturbed way and asked him to forgive her brother. They finished their meal quietly.

Charlotte and Tabby cleared the table. Anne stirred the fire. It was cold; November was fierce. The room grew a little darker all of a sudden. Anne turned to the window to have a look at the weather. She noticed a lightning strike. It had been abrupt and quick, but Emily had seen it too and her grey eyes opened wide.

She did not need to mention she was going out. Anne fetched her sister's cloak and lent her some gloves, for she herself had forgotten them in the morning and had regretted it.

Emily thanked her with a smile and whistled at Keeper, who was already at the door. Anne knew her sister would be gone for hours. She knew she did not need company other than Keeper's. She would often allow Anne to go along with her and they liked each other's presence, but the promise of the thunder was a call to freedom Emily could not ignore. And freedom, to her, was a lonely place. Anne respected that, closed the door behind her and watched her sister and her dog head for the moor quietly. She thought they were great companions. Soul mates. She thought Keeper would be the first to hear the next lines Emily would write down later in the day. Or the following night.

Anne smiled. She turned round and realised she was alone in the room. Charlotte was probably upstairs, reading or writing; Tabby was certainly busy with her tasks; her father was back in his study. He would go for a walk a few hours later, once the sky would be clear; Branwell would not be home before the middle of the night, leaning all his weight against Emily's arm; and Flossy was playing outside.

Anne felt crushed. Again, that corset. It was too tight, she thought. But it was also that room – too small. And that dress – too heavy. And that wind. Sometimes, that wind would be too loud.

CHAPTER 2

Winter had passed, as chilled and damp as its predecessors. March had been made of the same wet promises but had been more indulgent regarding the cold. The sky remained grey still, sometimes white, as white as snow. As though spring was too shy to make a proper entrance into their world.

Charlotte had read the Keighley newspaper to their father that morning, as she would most days, and was now trying to read and improve her French at the firelight. Yet Anne knew she had forced on her sight and now could not see a thing. She had set her tiny spectacles on the tip of her nose and approached the book so close that it was brushing it, but it was pointless. Her sister's sight was as catastrophic as their father's.

A surgery in Manchester had been planned for him. He was to leave in five months, and would most certainly stay there a while. A carriage would have to be ordered and it was a long journey. Anne thought Charlotte would need an operation too, someday.

It was warm in the dining room. And quiet. Peaceful. Flossy was snoring at Anne's feet. Emily had gone out with Keeper. It was dark and getting late. She would be hungry and thirsty when she would be back, Anne had thought. And therefore she had saved her the largest potato and buttered two pieces of bread for her. Emily was not an eager eater, but Anne feared that her sister was not in good health. She would never admit it to her – Emily always showed impatience when one would worry about her – and she knew her attempt at reminding her sister to eat would not be misunderstood. She had done it all the same.

Anne rested her head on her rocking chair. She liked lulling herself to sleepiness. And it was so warm… So tranquil…

Someone knocked at the door of the dining room. Anne jumped. Charlotte adjusted her glasses. They saw their father peeping through the door. He looked tired. The lines on his forehead looked a bit more deeply dug each year. Each month. As though they were announcing or reminding of an eternal change, an upcoming curse they would all have to deal with – the loss of their maker. An invisible hand was digging into their father's skin the way a gravedigger dug the earth. Anne feared and loved those lines. She suddenly realised how old her father was and how immense the gap between the two of them was. Two generations separated them and it felt like an entire life. His hair was so white and he had a fatigued look on his face. His hands were wrinkled too and he was still wearing his wedding ring that had grown to become a natural part of his body, a golden circular little limb.

He wished them good night and told them he was going to bed. He would use the same words every night and they would answer with the same ones, too.

He could not see well in the subdued room and his eyes stopped on blurry silhouettes, the ones he seemed to assume were his daughters'.

"Rest well, Papa," Anne softly said.

He gently closed the door and they heard him climb the stairs.

The front door suddenly opened and a rush of wind broke in the hall. Anne knew it was Emily and Keeper, back from their walk in the moor. Charlotte did not question it either; she had focused her eyes back on her reading and did not look up. Anne gently pushed Flossy aside, for she was lying on the top of her foot, and joined her sister in the hall. Keeper had already gone to the kitchen, probably to sip some water. Emily was taking off her cloak and asked if their father was asleep. Anne replied that he was. She said she had saved her dinner; she would warm it for her and feed Keeper while she was eating. Emily sighed. They went to the kitchen together and Anne served her sister. Keeper got his food and devoured it. Emily hissed at him. He turned to her and went back to his bowl less savagely.

Emily did not say she would fetch Branwell at the Black Bull pub; they both knew she would. The entire parsonage did and no one ever mentioned it. Anne knew there was nothing to say or do to convince her sister to leave their brother in his misery; she was, in fact, relieved every time she would hear they were back together. Charlotte had once told Emily that Branwell did not deserve such pity and she would have kept going if she had not seen the look on Emily's face. As for their father, he would rather have ignored his son's degradation. Anne knew it was too much to bear for him; she knew he felt powerless. Emily was their saviour.

The bell struck nine. Anne had heard Charlotte go to bed. Emily had not eaten her entire meal, had probably given half of it to the dog, but declared she was full. Anne told her she had completed another poem during the day. She did not need to ask her sister to read it; Emily smiled and Anne went up quietly to her room, trying not to wake Charlotte, who had gone to bed, to bring her notebook to her. Back down in the kitchen, she left it to Emily and whispered, "Thank you."

She left, knowing she would be given a kind compliment followed by advice and suggestions the next morning. Her sister would read it, once or twice only, before she would dig into her own poetry work. Anne knew Emily could daydream for hours before writing a line.

And then the time to bring Branwell back home would come. The other customers must know the entire process, too, Anne thought. And yet she was not sure any of them were ever of real help to her sister. If they had ever tried, Emily would have ignored them, no doubt.

Anne could imagine her sister looking through the window of the Black Bull, searching for their brother, finding him, coming in, hearing his deep and solemn oaths that sip should be the last and hearing all his unspeakable curses on his own head if he ever should fill another glass or hold another bottle[2], seizing his arm and getting out with him, the weight of his body and misery on her back and shoulders. She imagined them staggering to the parsonage, Branwell because he would not be in control of himself and Emily because she would try to be in control of both of them.

Anne suffered for her sister. She knew how Branwell sounded like, looked like, smelled like when he was in that state. Anne admired her. Emily was her heroin, more than just a sister. If Charlotte was the walls of the parsonage, Emily was the air they all breathed inside it.

Anne tried to lull herself to sleep. She knew her sister would rest very little. She knew Branwell would be unbearable, hateful and disgusting. She knew the next day would be the same as the one that was slowly ending. Yet she also knew she had things to write and that was enough for the night.

---

[2]*The Tenant of Wildfell Hall*, Anne Brontë

CHAPTER 3

They could always hear him, from the kitchen, the dining room and from upstairs. If they had not lived in such a high, remote place, their neighbours would have heard him, too. Branwell would raise his voice high[3], once back from the deafening confusion of jingling coins and loud curses[4] and toasts. Or when he was deadly tempted to return to that bustle, promising it was the last but one jaunt, the "just once more"[5] request for money he would make to his father. His discourse would sometimes stop making any sense at all, his emotions being too overwhelming, destructive, preventing all attempt at giving sensible talk.

Anne in those moments wished she could shut her eyes on her brother's faults, on his very heart that she long ago trusted and which proved itself less warm and less generous than she had thought it[6].

In those moments, Branwell would give them a specimen of his character[7] before spitting a tumultuous

---

[3]*The Tenant of Wildfell Hall*, Anne Brontë
[4] "
[5] "
[6] "
[7] "

"What can't be cured must be endured!"[8] to the mortified assembly.

In those moments, Anne wanted to cover her ears but would not surrender to such childish gesture. Charlotte would remain stoic, her eyes fixed on her book, but incapable of continuing reading. Emily's face would be grave, shut, and her movements to tame the dough would be firmer. Branwell would keep saying that he could not, that he could not stop, that he would not. He would keep talking about that woman in York, about how much he wanted to get back to her, how much he hated him, their father, or her husband, how much he hated that place. He felt like he was wasting his time, youth and talent there.

Branwell's words had been the same for weeks now. Anne could feel the muscles in her back and shoulders tighten every time her brother raised his voice. He was both unpredictable and predictably challenging, demanding and intolerable. When he did not succumb to one of those crises, Branwell would simply lose contact with the real, tangible world around him. He would either not be himself and incapable of recognising anyone, or be too exhausted by his own depravation.

Anne tried to calm him down several times, to help him contain his rage and hate for their father's sake by whispering what she thought were soothing words; but Branwell was sometimes unable to understand them, or the comfort his sister was trying to offer him. Emily helped, but her sense of self-respect was engraved so deeply in her

---

[8] "

that she would, at other times, use rough honesty and manners to shake their brother. But it would not do. Branwell shouted at her several times too, calling her names, and Emily would fight back, turning the household into a battlefield. Charlotte did not intervene; only her eyes would judge the situation and they were always filled with disgust and shame. Powerlessness and desperate love, too —Anne knew so.

Spring, therefore, ended with darker hues than she had expected. Yet, she had decided to enjoy the sight of the daisies timidly growing around the house, the smell of the wildflowers she would sometimes pick on the moor when the sun allowed it.

When summer came into their lives, it did not bring concrete heat but sound hope all the same. A London publisher had responded to them. Favourably. They had had to change their names and Anne could feel the bitter taste of that compromise at the back of her mouth, but their works were to be published. They were to become books – actual books. Her story, Agnes's story, would be read. If she was lucky still and she had been so far, it would be. Anne thanked God for such an opportunity. She devoted her time to corrections, following the publisher's advice, yet respecting her own opinion.

Charlotte's novel had not been accepted. Anne knew her sister enough and she knew about ambition enough to empathise with her disappointment – perhaps, even jealousy. She did not dare say a comforting word to her, fearing to hurt Charlotte's dignity. Yet Anne knew her sister would use that disillusion to continue writing and even produce something better. She simply needed time, that was all.

And time passed, as it always did. June did, offering its pretty lilac branches above some streets of the town; as did July, blowing warm breaths of wind to the back of their necks and more sunny opportunities to escape the loud, distressful conversations that would often occur in the parsonage.

When the time came to organise their father's and Charlotte's stay in Manchester, Anne kept her worry to herself. She was glad that Emily was staying home too, for how would she have managed Branwell and his extravagances on her own? Tabby was too old and weak to refuse him anything or to stand between him and the house door. Young Martha, poor girl, looked terrified every time Branwell crossed the room she was working in and seemed to rely on Emily to protect her in case of an outburst. But Anne was not afraid of her brother. She feared being hurt by witnessing his abject self, more than getting in his way or being shouted at by him.

Yet Branwell was nowhere to be found the morning their father and Charlotte left. And no one mentioned him. Anne thought he was recovering somewhere or heading for Keighley or Halifax, where he sometimes disappeared. The old priest did not say much. He leant on Charlotte's shoulder to get on the carriage, trusting her frail body as much as her tenacious soul; and Emily, Tabby and Anne watched them leave.

Anne slept on her own the following night. It was unusual for her to have so much space and though she was delighted, she could not sleep. She imagined the surgery, the tools the doctors would use, her father's eye being opened and studied as though it was not even his own, as though he could not feel a thing. Charlotte had promised that she would stay during the entire process. She had, Anne knew, kept her anxiety about the operation to herself. Perhaps, she feared the probability of a future one for herself too and intended to get ready for it.

Anne could hear the rain hitting the windowpanes with anger. Although Yorkshire rain could be unforgiving, she found comfort in its harshness that she had known forever and slowly abandoned herself to unconsciousness.

She was sleeping peacefully when someone knocked at the door. Anne woke in a jump, startled. Her heart was racing.

"Annie, open the door!"

Branwell was whispering. She jumped out of bed and staggered to the door, half asleep.

"Sweet Annie!"

He did not ask her to let him in. He rushed to her and, all of a sudden, she felt her brother's body crushed against hers. He was heavy and she gasped.

"Annie, sweet Annie…"

Branwell was holding her so tight she could almost feel her ribs crack.

"Bran… you're hurting me!"

"Oh, forgive me, my sweet Annie!"

He let her go and she stepped away from him. Her bones were fine, yet she had an unpleasant feeling. She had no idea when he had got back home.

"I'll tell you about the most wonderful dream I've just had! Oh, Anne, it was so beautiful!"

He was drooling and wiped his chin with his sleeve. Anne looked away. It was dark; she could not see his eyes, but she had seen him in that state so many times before she could easily imagine what he looked like. A beast, she thought. Not her brother.

"S-Si-Si' down," he stammered in a rush. "Let's sit on your bed, sweet Annie, just like we used to when we were young! Do you remember, sweet Annie, huh? Do you remember how happy we were? What incredible stories we used to write? I was a gifted child, wasn't I? Oh, you too, sweet Annie, of course! You too! Do you remember Angria and Gondal?"

Anne kept silent. She pushed him gently aside so she could close the door behind him. She feared he would wake the whole household.

Branwell could barely stand. He almost lost his balance when she moved him. He was now close to the window and Anne saw him accurately in the moonlight.

She had been right. A beast. His eyes were partially shut, the look in them was blank. He was breathing loudly through his open mouth, looking around him like an animal lost in a stranger's house. His hair was a mess. His smell was the same as other nights – intolerable. Seeing her brother not being her brother any more was distressful enough to Anne. Smelling him was worse.

The stench came from his lungs, his throat, the inside of him. It gave Anne the feeling that her brother was rotting inside. Or rotten already. The smell would linger, as it always did – in her room, on his clothes, his skin perhaps, on her too, surely.

She looked at Branwell's mouth. Those lips that had sipped his favourite poison a few hours before – they were the same as the ones that used to kiss her cheek as a child. How was that possible?

Anne had long stopped feeling pity for her brother. She knew he was deeply miserable; she knew his weaknesses and she had felt for him. But she was tired now.

Yet her lips moved to repeat her usual words and her arms reproduced the ever-same gestures.

She softly put her hands on his shoulders in an attempt to help him stand still. She then took his hands in hers, holding them tight. Branwell suddenly had one of those smiles that told her he no longer knew who she was. His left hand escaped hers and stroked her cheek clumsily. He was rarely brutal to her—yet *that* was worse than a slap. He approached his thirsty mouth to hers.

"Branwell."

Anne turned her face. His smile widened. He was looking at her with his head oscillating. His breath was sickening.

"Branwell," Anne repeated.

She put her hands on his cheeks, trying to cool him down. He was burning hot.

"Everything's movin'—"

"Let's have a seat. Let's sit in the chair. I'll help you—"

"No," he mumbled.

He pushed her hands away in a violent movement that took her by surprise and hurt her arms.

"You're the worst…"

Anne blinked. She knew those words were not her brother's; she knew they belonged to some monster hidden inside him. Yet she was always hurt when Branwell allowed such insults out, when he would allow that monster to speak out. It was his voice, after all, his mouth, his tongue. Her brother.

"Am I now?"

"A pain in the ass…"

Anne swallowed. She walked to the bed slowly and sat down on her open sheets.

"I didn't mean… No…"

Branwell had a movement with his hand, suggesting he did not mean what he had said. Or perhaps, he felt abandoned, alone and foolish, standing in a corner of the room. He laughed stupidly.

Anne was exhausted and drowsy. She needed to rest.

She looked up at her brother. He looked silly, trying to be forgiven for something he had already forgotten he had said, turning the words – she was the only one to remember – into a joke.

Anne was not cold-hearted; yet she could feel her eyes were ice on him. She had forgiven him so much and so often. She felt empty now. Not mad, not shocked, not disappointed. Being mad, shocked or disappointed implied that such a night would be new or unusual. It was not.

Branwell kept on smiling like an idiot. He joined her on the bed, walking unsteadily and almost tripped. Anne did not move.

"Annie. That dream!"

She was motionless.

"So colourful! They were there, too! Mama and Maria and Elizabeth... They were smiling, Annie, smiling at me... How gorgeous they were! They were like angels, Annie! They're angels!"

It was always the same dream. The same description. Anne never knew if he was telling her about a real dream he had had, or if he only wanted her attention, if he needed company, unable to be alone with himself. Or if he simply could not sleep.

He elbowed her, probably expecting a reaction. She had none. After a second or two, she turned to her brother and saw that beast's face again – his mouth was wide open, his eyes half shut and staring at the void. He felt her eyes on him and smiled at her.

"Go to bed, Branwell," Anne sighed.

"I... I promise, Annie, I did pay for 'em. I paid for 'em. They just wouldn't let me have 'em..."

"What now?"

"The pints, Annie! I did pay!"

"Oh, Branwell..."

Worry replaced fatigue immediately. What was he talking about now? What did he mean? Had he put himself in trouble again? Would it ever end? Had he paid for whatever he had consumed and had they refused to let him drink anymore because he was so drunk already? Or had they refused to serve him because he had no more money? They could not afford to have debts. In any case, it was not good.

"Branwell, you need to stop that!"

Anne seized her head in her hands. She was shaking. He kept silent, confused.

"I didn't do anythin' wrong…"

He sat closer to her and tried to get her attention with his hand on her arm. His movements were indecisive and inaccurate. She looked at him and kept her tears inside. He did not.

"You hate me."

Did she?

"No, I don't. Of course, I don't."

She gave no justification. No passion to her words. Why was he staying there? Could he not see she needed to sleep?

"You do. You do hate me. Everybody hates me… I'm a piece of shit. I know it, Annie. He hates me more than anyone… I'm such… I'm so miserable… She's gone… They're all gone…"

Anne remembered her love for her brother in a second. It rose in her chest – her instinct had awakened. Seeing him weep was unbearable. His tone was always heart-tearing and, by soothing his pain, Anne would aim at soothing hers too. Yet she felt weak every time she would give in and comfort him. Charlotte said she was.

"No one hates you, love. Absolutely no one."

Sometimes she did, though. And she was sure Charlotte did, too. Perhaps Branwell was right and their father did a little as well. Maybe even Emily. But hate was so mingled with love. Hate was desperate love. Their hate was made of love and the despair of not being able to help.

Anne wiped her brother's tears with the tip of her fingers. She had gentle, thin hands that would often soften Branwell's crises. He sniffed. He looked like a child.

"He's angry at me, isn't he?"

"He's not."

The words came out naturally. She did not know whether she truly meant them or if they escaped her mouth automatically. By force of habit.

"I never do enough, I'm never good enough… I was a gifted child, though. Ain't that right, Annie?"

"You were."

"He's mad. He's toxic. A lunatic! One day, I swear, I'll leave this place! I hate him. I hate them all! I hate that place. Oh, Annie, I do! Ah, what does he want from me? One day I'll fight him!"

Anne did not say a word.

"You can see how bad he is, can't you, Annie? You, of all people, with your clear eyes and pure heart, you must see that. Yes. One day I'll challenge him! I'll never be like him, I can't. Thank God I can't! I'll never be such a—"

"He's your father," Anne interrupted sharply.

"Damn him!"

Branwell stood up in a jump, vaguely punching the air. He was foaming now. Anne knew he was close to one of those attacks of his and she tried to soothe him. Her tone was calm and comforting when she whispered,

"It's all right. It's all going to be all right."

He snorted, rushed back to her and broke into tears in her arms. She held him tight, feeling his wet face on her neck.

Anne prayed. She prayed hard and quietly, begging God to show her brother mercy. He was not a bad person, she swore; he was suffering. Struggling. That was all. If the Lord could make his pains more bearable, Branwell would behave more kindly. He would be respectable. She knew it. She did not doubt it. His Christian heart would guide him. She promised God she was right; she gave her word. She silently vouched for her brother.

Yet, deep down, she secretly knew she was lying. She secretly knew Branwell was hopeless. They all were. Despite all that, Anne kept her thoughts out of reach from God, or so she tried with all her might. That, too, was hopeless. That too, she knew.

Branwell seemed calmer now. She gently made him look at her and wiped his tears again. There he was. Her brother. No longer a beast. It was profound misery that she could see in his eyes now. God, have mercy on him.

Branwell had kept his jacket on. Anne helped him take it off, as well as his shoes. When she stood back up, he was already asleep. He began snoring and she knew from experience that trying to wake him up was pointless.

Anne sighed. She did not feel like sleeping in the chair; she was so tired, after all. She tapped his face gently, then a little more harshly when she saw no change in him. Branwell would not wake up.

She had asked for Emily's help so often, to shake him and carry him to his own bed. But Anne felt reluctant to do it now. Emily looked so fragile those days, she needed to rest. Anne would not allow herself to disturb her. Besides, she knew that even her sister would not have been able to make their brother properly get up and walk to his bedroom. It would have been painful to watch.

And therefore, Anne helped Branwell lie down on her bed. She wrapped him up in her blanket with care. She really would have to sleep in the chair.

CHAPTER 4

The wind was hissing. It was the choreographer of the trees down there and the orchestra conductor of birds in spring. None were singing that day. It was only the wind. But that wind was made of secret words. Travellers and strangers did not speak its language. The wind only spoke to the people of Haworth.

Light was slithering softly into the world. The sky was made of the same promises as the day before and the day after, no doubt. The sun was rising gently, taking its time and enjoying the pleasure of being a mystery, as though any soul could ever doubt it would come eventually.

Haworth was waking. So was the parsonage.

Anne turned to her bed. Branwell was still asleep. He had been sick during the night and she had had to fetch the basin in haste. His shirt and her pillow were nonetheless covered in a little of it and smelled. Branwell had wept himself back to sleep after that and snored the entire night, preventing her from getting any good rest. She thought of what he had said. She wondered if he had been right, if she hated him.

Anne felt torn. She regretted having lied to God to protect her brother and she regretted lying to herself. She would usually rather accept the truth than comforting nonsense and believing that Branwell could be saved by quiet lies was nonsense indeed.

She often wondered what her sisters and she would become when God called their father back to Him. They clearly could not rely on Branwell to provide for them and any prospects of marriage for any of them three seemed unlikely. What would they do? Who would they be? Neither Charlotte nor Emily ever raised the question, yet Anne knew it should have been a matter of worry for them, too. Somehow, Charlotte would always find a way to make a living. Anne was more concerned about Emily. Throwing her out of that house that did not even belong to them would be like cutting the thin thread that was holding her to the material world. Would she survive it? Emily was clinging to a comforting routine and had gone so ill every time she had left it; what would occur if she had to leave it forever?

Their father must have been tormented by that idea as well, surely. He was old and the end of his life would be filled with turmoil and deep worry about them. Anne hated that. She sighed, realising she would have to wander among strangers again, teach, discipline and pretend she was someone she was not, unsure of what her station in the world was.

She slowly walked to the window and saw her reflection in the pane. She judged herself thin and very pale. Almost transparent. Her eyes were two glitters in the glass. She found her shoulders and chest narrow.

How strange. How come she looked so vulnerable and yet felt so strong? Could her fragile-looking frame really contain such intensity? An intensity she could feel in her relatives, too. Something that was specific to them, that defined them. She could see it in her father's piercing eyes, in Charlotte's decisive footsteps, hear it in Emily's firm tone. Even Branwell still had it in him. Anne knew it was still in him. Somewhere.

Her eyes moved to some other corner of the window and she perceived him, lying on his stomach, half of his face buried in her pillow.

She turned round and saw him with more accuracy. He looked so fast asleep. Where was he right now? she wondered. In what strange world was he imagining himself to be? Was he seeing her, that woman who had abandoned him? Was he dreaming of himself with her? Or was he reviving his previous night with his club at the pub? In her room? Would he remember his words, his behaviour? Would he lie, saying he did not? Would he tell the truth, saying the same?

Was he only recovering from the overuse of whisky? Of beer? Both? No, not whisky, Anne decided. He was infinitely worse after strong alcohol; his scenes were even more painful to witness. He had had beer.

Suddenly, Anne wondered. Was her brother naturally vicious? The word sounded rough indeed, even in her head; yet she would not censor herself again. She felt that it was better to depict people as they really were than as they would wish to appear[9] – or even as she would wish them to.

---

[9] Preface

Then yes. Branwell, perhaps, was evil. Was it the reason why he could not stop behaving in such a manner? Had he been born with vice in him? Where had it come from? Anne could not imagine a saner man than her father and her mother, poor soul, had always been described to her nearly as a saint.

Or was it all because of that woman? Had she transformed him? Sucked the nice, smart, strong Branwell out of himself? Had she used him really, never loved or even considered him?

Or was it because of herself? She was the one who had convinced her employers to trust Branwell for the tutor's position, after all. Was all of that her fault? Was she the cause of her own brother's degradation?

Anne pondered. She took a while to find the right answer. She would neither excuse herself blindly nor accuse herself wrongly. No more hypocrisy.

No, Anne thought. Her brother had long been unhappy. He had lived his youth in frustration, waiting for something great to come to him. And nothing had. He had talent; he had been a gifted boy. All was gone now. He was a sombre adult man whose heart had been broken and who had wasted his young years waiting for his talent to grow, to be detected by the great and recognised.

Anne realised nothing would come out of him now. It seemed obvious. Her sisters and she were the ones who were using the talents God had given them, not him. How could he be in such a state?

Maybe there was still hope, though. Maybe Branwell could be saved. Saved from himself. Healed.

But no… No more hypocrisy, she had decided.

Anne felt weary. Every time she would indulge in such thoughts to invade her mind, she would end up answerless and tired. She could not allow herself to be. Work needed to be done.

She got dressed, whispered her morning prayers, thanking God that He gave her the strength to ignore painful interrogations and joined Emily and Tabby downstairs.

As soon as she came into the kitchen, her sister gave her a note. Anne knew it was her comments on another poem she had asked her to read. She smiled. Those notes were like secrets they would share. She had no doubt Emily had proved herself honest without being cruel, respectful without being subjective. She would read the note later, after tea, when she would work on her writing.

Anne took a seat at the kitchen table and drank her tea quietly. She felt tired and guessed the day would be slow.

She looked around pensively. The walls were white and refreshing. They gave her a feeling of comfort and clarity, but also cold. Clean white walls, perhaps, were a lure. They gave an illusion of peace of mind and honesty. As if their home had nothing to hide, as if they all lived orderly lives, as if they hid no lie, no mystery, no secret ambition or a feeling of lifelong mourning.

The kitchen was filled with the smell of newly washed sheets hanging above her head. Tabby had already swept the floor and it looked dry and clean. Healthy. She was humming a song she had taught them when they were children, a song only Yorkshire peasants could understand.

Her words and accent made them laugh when they were young and cheeky, Anne remembered. She smiled. Branwell was the one who would tease Tabby with the least pity. She remembered his eyes, full of childish impertinence. He was always forgiven, though. Their aunt, bless her soul, Anne thought, their aunt would always forgive him. So would Tabby. So would she, she realised. Maybe not their father.

Yet Anne felt a rush of tender compassion rise in her. She admired her father. She did. She would never admit it to Branwell, but she knew that he had gone through so much. His heart seemed dry, for his eyes were; yet, he had overcome losses, prejudice and various life difficulties and challenges she and her siblings had only a vague idea of. Oh, she had lost much, too. The faces of her mother – the one she imagined her to have had at least – of Maria, Elizabeth, of her aunt, of him, travelled in her mind like little flying portraits. She seized them mentally, one by one, and had a silent prayer for each of them.

"Why, you sure look dreamy this morning, Anne," Tabby noticed.

She said it without looking at her. She must have had one of her quick glances at her and made the remark once focused on her task again.

Anne caught the hint. She stood up, seized a cup of tea, filled it with the warm beverage and repeated her usual mission to wait for her father. Back in the kitchen, she fed the dogs and filled a bucket with water to help with the washing up.

Fatigue made her a little dizzy. It was not unpleasant, though.

She had used that same bucket to wash Branwell once. And that same bucket also reminded her of the basin she had fetched during the night. His spasms were insufferable when he would get sick. She shook her head.

The water was freezing. Her hands would need hours to get warm again. She finished with the dishes and dried them.

Someone knocked at the door. The postman, Anne thought. And then she remembered.

She looked up at Emily, who caught her glance of worry and frowned. Tabby left to answer the door.

Anne could feel her sister's eyes on her. She knew she would not stop staring until she told her what she had in mind. Anne gulped. She thought of her father, who, had he been there, would certainly have heard the doorbell ring and who would have been waiting to know who was calling. He would have been disappointed and ashamed. Worried, again. Surely and despite it all, it was a blessing that he was away.

Anne dropped the dishtowel and hurried to the door. Emily quickly caught her arm.

"He said he had paid for them, but I'm not sure... He was so..."

Without a word, Emily rushed out of the kitchen and Anne heard her determined footsteps in the corridor and hall. She felt frozen. It was the third time that month. Anne thanked God that Charlotte and her judgemental eyes were absent.

She joined her sister and Tabby at the door. The old servant's expression was cold. She was staring at the three men standing on the threshold with their rude hands – hateful claws – open in front of them, looking like they were waiting for the money they were owed. She had a hard face, being so loyal to them. To Branwell.

Emily did not look up at the men. She simply asked, "How much?" They replied in their coarse voices. Branwell... Anne thought in despair. She was ashamed, her arms folded around her chest, her hands clenched to the fabric of her dress.

Emily seized her cloak and emptied her pockets. She counted her coins. It did not seem there were enough of them and Anne immediately searched in her own purse. She had saved that money for paper and had already spent the one she had planned to use for ink the last time other men knocked at the door and waited with their filthy hands open.

Anne gave her own coins to Emily, who gently squeezed her hand when she took it. The men received their money and before leaving, said, "You better watch 'im, miss. Some men ain't as nice as us."

Emily glared at them. Keeper barked at her feet. She was wearing her dress covered in subtle lightnings and her eyes were full of them when she looked at the one who had pronounced those words quite straightforwardly. Neither Anne nor Tabby dared say a word.

"If my brother ever gets in trouble again, with you, with anyone else, send someone here and call on me. If you don't and if my brother gets hurt, I will consider you responsible."

The men blinked but kept silent. Emily could barely ever speak to strangers. Yet that morning she did, did not wait for an answer and slowly shut the door. Tabby took her cloak and Anne's purse in her arms and hung them without a word. Anne knew she was worried. That visit had made her gloomy.

Emily froze in front of the door of her father's study. She seemed to ponder, then turned to Anne and Tabby and said, "When he is back… Not a word."

CHAPTER 5

When Anne's father and Charlotte returned to Haworth, the wind felt chillier and chillier on their way to the top of the hill on which the parsonage stood. The rain kept pouring. The hesitating warmth had quickly been replaced by a prompt and firm expectation of autumn, making the place look as gloomy as could be. Not to mention that even through the thick raindrops, Anne could see the tombstones lying in the graveyard facing the house and sometimes felt surrounded by death more than life.

They had received Charlotte's letter mentioning their date of arrival and the four women had prepared fresh beds and a hot meal. Then, Anne had seized her father's hands in hers, which were warm and gentle, while Emily had greeted them roughly, hiding her concern for their father deep in her heart but inspecting his eye and appearance nonetheless. She had grabbed their trunks and brought them to the parsonage. Tabby had welcomed them with a large smile, showing the absence of several teeth at the front of her mouth. No one had asked about Branwell.

"Don't you think I know, Anne?"

Anne looked up from her book. They had had a pleasant evening the day before, glad to be reunited despite Branwell's absence and their father's condition, and Anne had had a good night's sleep. Her brother had not dared trouble her in the presence of Charlotte in the bedroom.

Yet, the next morning, Charlotte looked at her above her spectacles. Her eyes were accusing. She had that same elder-sister tone she would use with them when they were children and had done something she would find reprovable.

Anne did not look away.

"Don't you think I know he did it again? And keeps doing it. Those rude men saw me leaving the church this morning and they came to me. They stopped me in the middle of the street, asking me for money. People were staring, Anne. I had never felt so ashamed in my entire life—"

"You led them here, then," Anne interrupted in a neutral voice, remembering the look on her father's face that morning when he closed the front door behind him while she was on her way to deliver him his tea.

"Of course, I didn't mean to worry our father. I had no money. What else could I do? They wouldn't let me go. If I hadn't been the local vicar's daughter—"

"Who were those men?"

"Workers. From Bridgehouse Mills, surely. They still smelt like beer and their eyes were – they were expressionless."

"I'm sorry you got frightened, Charlotte."

Anne's sister's jaws clenched with dignity.

"I was more grieved than frightened. Even if I had had money on me, I wouldn't have given them any. I will not pay for someone else's outrageous mistakes."

"Then who will? If none of us does, who will?"

"He will! He must! Wouldn't you say it encourages him that we do? If he never pays for his behaviour, if he always gets away with it, don't you think he'll never learn to be ashamed? He keeps proving himself childish and foolish; perhaps, he needs to be treated like a child or like a fool."

Charlotte's words seemed pitiless, yet Anne knew they were triggered by pain and imprinted with reason. They were like wells – threatening and filled with tears she would not let out.

"I can't even begin to imagine what he owes so much money on. Or on how much of it. The sum they demanded was – extravagant."

Charlotte took off her glasses and cleaned them with the sleeve of her dress.

"He could have saved that money he owed for paper. He could have sent letters, replied to some employment advertisements. He could have—"

Anne leant towards her sister and squeezed her tiny hand in an attempt to comfort her.

"He needs to heal first. He needs to get better," she whispered.

Charlotte composed her face again. Her eyes seemed smaller behind her glasses. For a second or two, Anne was amazed at her sister's gigantic nature locked in such a fragile-looking frame. She had a driving force in her. She was a leader who had no idea she was a leader.

Anne's bond with Charlotte was more subtle, a little more timid, than her bond with Emily. The affection they had for one another was based on mutual trust and respect. It was more mentally conducted than her love for Emily. She and the latter would often be mistaken for twins. Anne could see her physical resemblance with Emily, but she was aware that people made that common assumption mainly because she and her sister would never part once in society. They looked stuck to one another.

Charlotte was different – stronger in a way. She could survive on her own; Anne was sure of it. She was shy and reserved, but content among small assemblies. She listened and observed before she trusted; her path amid hosts or guests was a long and narrow one. Yet she did not need the constant presence of any one of them to make acquaintances or even lifelong friends.

Charlotte was contradictory, Anne thought. Her voice was sometimes barely louder than the twittering of an ensnared bird; other times she would arm herself with courage, look one in the eye and speak for the three of them.

Emily was happy at home. She had rarely ever left it. She belonged to the moor, the sky, the quiet of the house and the deafening words in her head.

As for herself, Anne had the courage to leave and make her way in the world. It had been desolate sometimes – lonely. She had not had the choice to do otherwise then, but she took pride in having done it on her own nonetheless, organised her own departure and earned her own money. Oh, it had not been much and the families and children could be difficult, but she still had seen a bit of the world. Through the spectrum of a governess – yes. But Anne had

had a quick taste of life. She had found the world harsh and violent, but also comforting and colourful at times. She even rejoiced in the new company, discovering new faces and listening to unfamiliar voices. She had proved herself useful, needed and trustworthy. She had brushed new intimacy. She had had enough self-confidence to praise her brother to her employers. She had felt happy and impatient to share her new life with Branwell, to mingle her former and new selves, to have a familiar and cherished face around. She had been proud of herself for having been the one without whom her brother would not have had a profession. And he—

They had to leave in such a hurry. Branwell had cost her her independence. Anne wondered if she was secretly still resentful towards him. She had been so ashamed…

She turned to Charlotte. She wanted to tell her that she understood. She wanted to tell her that she knew how hurt she was, how worried, how helpless she felt! How degrading it was to see Branwell destroying himself in such a manner. How she wondered if it would ever stop, if they would ever be well again.

The words almost slipped from her mouth and tickled her lips. But she said, "I know you are disappointed."

Charlotte looked up at her. She squeezed Anne's hand back. Anne felt the warmth of her sister's skin. She had been right: Charlotte was wildly alive and could survive anything. Anne smiled at her.

Charlotte was writing and Anne noticed ink stains here and there on her childlike hand.

"Are you writing to Miss Nussey? Mrs Gaskell?" she asked to change the subject and soothe her sister.

Charlotte cleared her throat.

"No," she replied simply.

She slid her pages to the other end of the dining table and sighed.

"Save your money for yourself, Anne. Branwell is ill with a disease that empties the most filled purses. Emily won't listen... Please do."

Anne was reflecting on what answer to give her sister, but the door suddenly opened and Branwell appeared. His eyes were swollen and his cheeks red. He looked like himself nevertheless. It was a relief – a tired version of himself, but their brother all the same.

Yet Anne felt Charlotte tense beside her. She was looking at Branwell directly for once. She had not seen him in weeks.

"Don't you have a wash now and then?" she asked him.

Her tone was not dry, but her voice was firm. Anne let go of her hand and they both stared at their brother. He looked powerless, pitiful. He ignored Charlotte.

Anne could feel the tension between them three. It was an invisible guest, a fourth person in the room. She chose to protect the old man studying across the hall.

"Do you mind closing the door, Branwell? Flossy's all muddy; I don't want her to come in here," Anne gently said.

Branwell looked at her. Anne's face was too gentle for her not to be obeyed. He slowly shut the door and made a movement as if to say, *"Et voilà!"*

"Sorry I slept in your bed several nights, Anne," he then whispered.

Anne sighed. So Branwell had decided to be provocative that day. Charlotte gasped.

"Where did *you* sleep?" she asked with astonishment.

"I slept fine," Anne replied.

Charlotte glared at her brother. Her eyes were swords. There, Anne thought, he had crossed the line.

"Aren't you ashamed—"

"I—" he began. "I said I'm sorry."

He looked unsteady. He was hesitating, Anne could see. In the end, he was unsure of wanting to make a scene – again – and could, perhaps, feel as well as Anne that he had crossed an invisible line, too.

"Oh, you're sorry, aren't you? Do you think it's fair that your sisters should pay for the consequences of your actions? Do you think it's right to occupy your younger sister's bed and prevent her from sleeping properly? Don't you have any principles at all? What sort of a brother are you? What sort of a *man* are you?"

"Charlotte—"

Anne grasped her arm. Branwell covered his ears with the palms of his hands.

"Aren't you responsible enough to hear the truth, Branwell? Can't you be honest with yourself and brave? Will you hear that you shamed yourself again last night, and all of us, that Papa this morning, because I wouldn't, had to pay, literally, for your extravagances to save you from going to jail because of all your debts?"

Charlotte was fiery. She had stood up and her tiny figure was filled with rage. She was a mountain. Anne had to let go of her arm. She had left her chair, too, but felt so little, so young. The powerless, youngest sister again.

Branwell was on the verge of tears. He looked drunk once more. He suddenly screamed and challenged their sister with all his size, all his masculinity. Anne found him repulsive. Charlotte did not look down for a second, nor did she step back. They were like wolves.

"Emily!" Anne cried.

Branwell struck the dining table with his fist and then hit Charlotte on the back of her head. He had not used all his strength, far from it; yet the two women gasped. They stared at their brother, speechless. A minute passed.

All of a sudden, Charlotte reacted and slapped him. The noise the gesture made seemed to echo in the room, in their heads. Anne covered her mouth with her hand. Branwell looked shocked. They were used to fighting quite often as children – as two passionate, wayward souls – yet the innocent, playful, silly aspect of their old quarrels could not apply to the one that was taking place that day, in front of their younger sister's eyes. They were now two adults wrestling, a grown man hitting a woman who had chosen to fight back.

"Now," Charlotte said in a low voice, as astonished at her reaction as her siblings. "Have you recovered from your excesses of last night?"

Her large eyes were spitting fire. Branwell stroked his cheek.

Then, an access of rage and violent masculine pride seized him and he grasped Charlotte by the fabric of her dress. She was no longer a mountain; she suddenly looked like a rag doll and confusion and fear invaded her face. Anne screamed.

"No! No, stop! Emily!" she yelled.

She succeeded in making Branwell let go of their sister. His arm tried to find a new grip, however, and seemed to search for Charlotte's neck.

He found it. Branwell pushed his sister to the wall. There was a noise. A breath lost in the air, a gasp. Charlotte's eyes were wide open; the shock had made her blind.

Finally, Emily rushed in. She flew to them, her hair wild and her expression shut. She had just returned from the moors, surely, and the strength she always borrowed from them allowed her to make Branwell step back and let go of Charlotte. Emily then stood between them, protecting her sister with her body and deterrent presence and slapped their brother with all her might. He tripped. All of them had their father's piercing eyes and when Branwell met Emily's, he flinched.

"Charlotte—"

"Leave," Emily interrupted in a strict whisper.

Branwell left the room. The three sisters remained frozen for a minute, or, perhaps, five or ten. None of them said a word. Anne realised she had forgotten to breathe.

After a while, Emily asked, "What did he do to you?"

Charlotte was unable to reply. Emily then turned to Anne and their eyes understood each other.

"I know," Anne whispered. "Not a word."

CHAPTER 6

The incident was never mentioned between them. Branwell honoured his family with his presence at dinners and kept out of the pub for several nights.

Yet Anne felt tense and could not sleep well. A line had been crossed – a border, a world, perhaps. Hate and suffering had taken control of them. Anne feared it would never be the same.

It was stupid, though. It had not been the same since their return from Thorp Green, since Charlotte's from Brussels. They had lived separate lives for a while, had gone through experiences that had left marks on their hearts – marks they could not guess or understand in each other.

On the day following the incident, Emily made Branwell talk and repeated his words to Anne. First, Branwell maintained he had no recollection of the previous night, of his deeds or others'. But Emily was fierce and impatient and she threatened her brother to fetch testimonies of the night elsewhere. After a while, after quantities of semi-confessions, Branwell told her a story his sister already knew by heart and admitted he had had a fight at the Black Bull. First sober, he had been silent and glum. Then, Branwell's little club, who found him an unfailing source of merriment to them when he had something in him[10], had encouraged him to order gin. Animal rivalry had eventually risen among the men, as it would often do when alcohol was a member of the jaunt and all the little tribe had bet on Branwell's opponent, which had made Branwell angry. It had all been a game at first, a silly one, but they had drunk a great deal and the game had suddenly become less stupid and more dangerous. Yes, he had had a lot of beer, too... Mr Thompson, the owner of the Black Bull, had stopped them, threatening to throw them out of his pub and never allow them in again. The three men who had bet against Branwell had claimed their due in pints. Afraid of starting the fight again and being expelled from his favourite place forever, Branwell had accepted. Yet he had spent most of his money on his own drinks already and had been unable to pay for all the other men's, resulting in what they had considered "interests" and a large sum of money he had then owed them.

Branwell then swore he did not remember telling them where he could be found during the day. Emily countered that he obviously had, as he always did. She told Anne Branwell had burst into tears in the end, exhausted. She did not add that she had given him a wash and clean clothes, but Anne guessed when their brother sat at the dinner table looking fresh and smelling like soap.

Over the course of the days that followed the never-mentioned incident, Anne felt a change in herself. There was a time when she believed her brother and her family

---

[10]*The Tenant*

could climb the mountain of difficulty they were facing. Perhaps, that mountain was just a hill that required strength of mind and will. Perhaps, that mountain had been planted by God to challenge their bonds to one another and their morality.

Perhaps Branwell was being punished for his relationship with a woman who had since long sworn before God she would forever belong to another. Perhaps, Anne was too, for she had introduced him to her. Perhaps, it was her mission to save her brother.

Yet Anne could not imagine such an unforgiving deity that would rule with such tyranny. Plus, she could see the self-centredness in believing she was the one who had to lead her brother to salvation. She rejected that idea.

No. Charlotte was right. As she often was. Branwell was the only one who should pay for Branwell's behaviour and the only one who could save Branwell. She had to ignore that sense of guilt; it was unfair to herself and it made her narcissistic.

The time when she would have faith in her brother had gone. It had been a sweet cloud of hope made of comfort and patience. But it had flown away. Anne was slowly becoming conscious of it. It was painful. Perhaps it had vanished when she wondered if her brother had vice in him, if he was naturally vicious. Perhaps it had gone long ago.

Or perhaps, it had never been there in the first place and she had kept her fingers crossed out of luck without truly believing her brother could change – be saved.

Anne did not believe he could be saved. He could not be saved. They could not.

She repeated the words to herself in a murmur, as an epiphany.

Of course, he could not. None of them had the slightest idea how to help him and it did not seem like Branwell wanted to be helped.

What did he want? What was he trying to do? Did he intend to drown in all the drinks he was having? Drown his former hopes, former love, current pain? Was drink a real solace to his care[11]? Was he trying to forget? Become someone else? Ignore his suffering by covering it with litres of liquor?

Did he want to die young and remain known for his – unfinished – work and as a desperate artist, like the tragic hero of a French novel? Was it his sick way to become immortal?

Anne did not understand her brother. She pitied him and wished she could have spared him all the sufferings in the world, been a shield for him. Yet, no, she could not understand him. He was a man, the only son in their family and all the doors were open to him. So many had been as soon as he was born, for the simple reason of his sex. He had studied, been faced with opportunities she or her sisters had never dared conceive for themselves, with options of careers that they as women could only skim, mimic, or copy unofficially. He was wasting all his chances.

Anne could remember how cherished he had been as a child, how well he had been treated. The gifted boy. He

---

[11] *The Tenant*

had been so free, so many times forgiven, so loved. It had been done in a quiet manner and she had been too, yes, as well as Charlotte and Emily; but Branwell, for his noticed talent and gender, had been distinguished.

But, perhaps, too much love could be a burden. A weight. Perhaps even a rope around the neck.

For a minute, Anne tried to picture herself in Branwell's position. She failed, for she found that Branwell lacked that sustaining power of self-esteem which leads a person[12]. She could simply not feel what he could feel. Was she lacking empathy?

Then, she imagined him as a novel character. She would have had to create a history around him, an environment, experiences, all sorts of reasons, all sorts of paths that would have led her protagonist to his acquired personality or wrong choices.

Anne closed her eyes and then could see. There. There he was – her evil, weak, so very human character. There he was, her brother. She had to change some bits of his appearance to see him more clearly. She made him more handsome, painted his auburn hair blond and thickened his lips.

There he was. Standing in front of her, gazing. That was how she imagined the real Branwell to be. That was him, truly him. That constant air of mockery, that attitude of nonchalance, that eternal youth, or rather that obvious refusal to let youth go…

12"

She had painted him. She opened her eyes. Branwell appeared to her as clearly as Emily, who was coming back home accompanied by Keeper barking and whom she could see through the window.

It was raining and muddy out there and Anne heard Tabby rush to the door as fast as her ageing body allowed her to – she must have heard Keeper despite her worsening hearing, Anne thought – to prevent the dog from entering and making a mess in the entire parsonage. Anne noticed that even one-third of Emily's dress was covered in mud. Where on earth had the two of them been?

No one would ever ask, however. Emily never gave a clear answer and they all knew she and Keeper could go far.

Emily.

Anne wondered if her sister had always known that Branwell was a lost cause. She wondered if she had given up on him before any of them had if that was why she was so patient and forgiving with him. Perhaps she knew there was nothing better to expect from their brother.

Anne shuddered. What a terrible thought. The words in her head still felt like thorns in her chest, she was not ready to let them roam freely in herself yet. But she realised she might have caught something there. After all, Emily would sometimes deliver truths that none of them had even conceived and they were often puzzled before admitting to themselves that she was right. Her truths could be unwelcome first, but they always conveyed their own morals to those who were able to receive them[13]. Pitiless Emily challenged them.

Perhaps she had kept that truth to herself because she had known it would have been too upsetting for her, Charlotte and their father. Perhaps she had kept it a secret, a burden she could be the only one to carry.

For a second, Anne saw her sister as a soothing presence and a constant observer of their family. She was never judgemental, never cruel. She had the quickest mind – Anne knew, for they had long dreamt and written together – an uncommonly strong and unique sense of morality and she could often be seen by strangers as cold or distant. And now and then she would allow out of her mouth the most honest realities in a distinct voice. Anne was conscious of the fact that her sister was usually misunderstood or even unappreciated, but she was also certain of Emily's superiority in understanding the ones who could not understand her and the things none of them would ever be able to.

Then yes, she must have known. That entire time.

Branwell and Emily shared a sensitivity that they both must have felt as too intense, which had built a wall between them and the rest of the world. A sensitivity Charlotte and she could feel in themselves, too; but that they could keep quiet, at the surface, when necessary.

It seemed to Anne that Branwell sometimes needed to drain himself, just like bloodlettings would do, from

---

[13]Preface

suffocating emotions. From a suffocating world. Perhaps he had his own toxic way of doing it.

Anne heard Emily going directly upstairs, certainly to get changed. Tabby would wash her muddy dress later, or surely her sister would insist on doing it herself to spare the old servant.

Anne felt very much alone all of a sudden. Charlotte was locked in her room; so was Branwell. She had been very silent since the events and was certainly covering pages and pages with ink – that too, perhaps, was a way to drain oneself, Anne thought. Her father was revising his sermon for the next day and not a soul was allowed in his study when he was. Keeper was still barking in the yard, desperate to be let in. Flossy was snoring gently in front of the fireplace, unperturbed by the noise her furry friend was making. She had stolen from the sofa a cushion she was well-aware she was not allowed to use and was lying on it. Anne smiled at her cheekiness and did not wake her to scold her. She would have to when she woke up.

She thought of that man again. That Branwell. Who did not look like Branwell and who yet could never be mistaken for someone else in her eyes. He was the Branwell who was hiding in her brother's frame. The Branwell that poisonous liquids could let out. The Branwell who had replaced the gifted boy. The Branwell she did not like.

Anne needed to breathe. She was suffocating. It was suddenly too hot; perhaps, Tabby had placed too much wood in the chimney. She felt so tight in that dress. The fabric was so heavy and the collar was so close to her neck.

How did she manage to move or even breathe, usually? And who was the devil who had invented corsets? She needed some fresh air.

Anne walked out of the dining room as quietly as she could. She did not want Flossy to wake up, alarmed, and accompany her. She went up to her bedroom to fetch her notebook, sketchbook, pen and pencil. Perhaps she would write or sketch a portrait of that arrogant, nonchalant blond man who seemed to be staring at her from her own mind.

Anne walked by Branwell's room. The door was open and no sound could be heard from the landing. Her room was closed and she really needed to go out and visit the moors again.

It was very quiet, though.

Anne came closer to her brother's room. She hesitated and then peeped inside.

Branwell was lying on his bed. His body looked strange, as though dislocated. One of his hands was resting on his stomach, the other was holding what at first sight seemed to be a bottle. Anne looked more closely, for she had no idea how or when Branwell had managed to get any liquor. He had in the past kept a bottle of gin in his room, holding it off and on, abstaining one day and exceeding the next[14]. But it appeared not to be that eventually. The thing was made of glass but had an unfamiliar shape.

Anne was not acquainted with such an object, but the yellowish aspect of it did not make it look healthy. In fact, it looked quite repulsive. And Anne thought, if Branwell

---

[14]*The Tenant*

was clenching to it that way, it could not be good. Could it be what she thought it was? What she had once read about the famous Coleridge?

Branwell was fast asleep. His mouth was open and he still had his spectacles on. How pale he looked! A spectre! He almost seemed—

Anne could not think of the word. She looked around her brother and realised how unkempt and gloomy his room was. Papers and books were lying everywhere on the wooden floor, as well as plates that must have been there for days, long before Branwell had started to have his meals at the dinner table with them again – plates that were still half full and candles that had half burnt. The shutters were open, yet the room was dark. The walls had originally been light-coloured; they looked damaged now, as though Branwell had polluted them with his breath or sheer presence. The clothes that were hanging above his bed and the sheets looked overused and dirty and Anne wondered if the smell that had found a way to her nose came from them. The floor and carpet were dusty. The pages that were flooding them were covered in sketches and lines. All of them seemed to have been executed in haste and almost angrily. Anne knew that feeling – she herself was full of words, emotions and thoughts which sometimes begged to be let out. But she doubted Branwell's writings made any sense at all. There were ink stains on each page and all seemed to have been thrown onto the floor as soon as they had been filled, as if the plan was to have no plan at all, but rather to empty his mind.

The room looked cramped. It was a mess. Tabby and Martha must have been forbidden to come in and clean it. It was the room of a tormented soul. A room one wanted to flee.

Anne left. She should not have entered. She regretted she had. The door was usually shut and she had not come in for ages. So, she thought, that was Branwell's world, then. A little chaos.

She walked out and entered in Charlotte's and her own bedroom, which looked so neat and cosy, and grabbed her writing and sketching supplies. When she got back downstairs, she seized her cloak and bonnet, and left.

Anne's nature was not originally calm. She had learnt to appear so by dint of hard lessons and many repeated efforts.[15]

What a relief, then, to close the front door behind her and feel the wind in her hair, on her face. It was an icy wind for October, a pitiless one, the sort of wind that challenged one's determination to live in quite a high place. Anne accepted the dare and dove into the air with resolution and a steady step.

There, finally. Finally, she could breathe.

The way to the moors felt short. As soon as her foot stepped on the familiar moss and rocky hills, as soon as it brushed the pale and pink heathers and rebellious bracken, Anne was unwound.

The sky was snowy white; no cloud was disrupting it. The puddles around Anne reflected the light of the sky; so its light.

---

[15] *The Tenant*

The moors were cold and unwelcoming again today, Anne thought. It seemed they did not wish to be disturbed in their chilly tranquillity; they wanted to be left alone. Wild and untouched.

Anne promised to respect their need and follow their laws. She vowed to remain a peaceful intruder.

The hills that lay ahead looked like mountains, for they were still far. Each time she would climb them and get to the top of them, Anne was astonished to see that the landscape behind her repeated itself before her.

The moors were vast, endless. Infinite. They had no beginning, no end. Absolute pleasure could be found in tricking the paths that generations of humans, shepherds and wanderers had traced. Emily had once told her that walking the paths that violated the moors was disrespecting them. Paths were meant for human worlds or for quiet visits to the woods with city-dwellers. They did not belong in the northern moors.

The herd of sheep had been distanced. The paths were becoming fewer. The moor was presenting itself slowly, shy, as though Anne was a stranger.

But they had long been friends, maybe sisters. Anne had hiked its hills countless times, taken breaks at its quiet ponds a hundred times. Nothing was unknown and yet everything was. The persisting dew on the lush, brownish hills; the thistles resting under blankets of melting autumn snowflakes; the teasing rocks and stones that tested human's capacity and tenacity to go any further; the empire-looking world that included no borders and would not let Anne, or any other human soul, conquer it.

The moor could be at peace; Anne did not wish to rule. Her heart was made of a purer ambition.

She ran down the hill she had just climbed. That one had challenged her physical abilities and she had had to untie her bonnet to catch her breath. Her hair had been freed by the unforgiving wind that seemed to be mad at her for being so intrusive and to try push her back to where she had come from and was flying loose. For once, Anne did not care to look proper. Propriety did not exist on the moors. The rules were different there. Or perhaps there were none.

She noticed a comfortable-looking rock covered in moss that she decided to use as a cushion. Her pad, steel pen and pencil had not been a pleasure to carry all the way from the parsonage, but they would prove to be of use now.

Anne first made a quick sketch of the man who had not left her mind. She tried to express the teasing aspect she could guess in him, focusing on his eyes and posture. In the end, she found him rather good-looking, well-executed and singularly, dangerously attractive. He was the sort of man all the young ladies in the neighbourhood would surely aim at attracting; the sort of man she would want to escape from.

He could be a character. And a character implied a story. The usual questions effortlessly popped into her busy mind. What would the story be? What seemed to be that dangerous, beautiful character's universe? What did she need to say?

The truth. Always the truth. Reality. What was reality at the moment?

The name emerged in her mind quickly. Branwell. Branwell was her reality. That character had always been

Branwell, after all. What could Branwell's new story be? Who did he seem to be? Who was he when none of them, not even Emily, was around? What could he do?

Anne remembered her feeling of despair earlier in the day when she first thought of a bottle when noticing the object her brother was holding. She remembered the pain, the disappointment, the hopelessness. The hate. Yes, the hate. It was easier to see it now that it was all meant to be hidden in a story.

Yet she could not build this story from that man's point of view. His was not the one she knew too well, nor was it the one she felt most interested in. It had to be a distant point of view. But not too distant. The point of view of someone who would be distant enough to dislike him, to see the evil in him and close enough to know, love and blame him. The point of view of a woman. The point of view of a wife.

CHAPTER 7

How could it be dark already? Hidden amid the hills, so small and insignificant among the green, the grey and the brown, Anne had believed herself invisible and protected from the coming of the night.

It was approaching, however. Softly, quietly, as if not to disturb her. Soon enough, there would be no light for her to keep writing and to go back to the parsonage peacefully.

Anne sighed and closed her book with regret. She had used the last minutes she could steal from slithering night and it was now time to admit she would never win against nature.

She found her way back home quite easily, although her mind was full of words and images that urged her to be set free and to rest on paper. It felt like she had trapped herself in her own book when she had closed it. How impatient she was to be home!

Finally, she arrived in town. It was completely dark now and Anne was the only human soul stepping on the fresh and humid cobbles of Haworth streets. She was walking at quite a quick pace. Oh, she was not afraid of the dark; she was too sensible for that. And the folkloric ghost stories Tabby used to tell them about gypsies and wild northern creatures had long ceased to frighten her.

She was walking fast because the words in her head were not getting any quieter and she was worried that she would be late for dinner. If she happened to be, her father would not be pleased. "Self-respect also lied in self-discipline." And respect for others had always implied to be on time for dinner to her poor-and-hungry-rooted Irish father.

Anne walked by the church. She looked up, but it was too dark for her to see what time it was. Yet she was not far now.

Soon, it began to rain, and shy drops were slowly being replaced with more assertive ones. Anne quickened her pace again.

She noticed the familiar gate and imposing, strict-looking parsonage. It seemed so bleak to her suddenly, so imposing and high, so strange, almost airy. All the dwellings nearby had seemed perfectly traditional and common on her way up there. She had paid no attention to them and had known them forever. Yet, it was her own home that was stunning her at that particular moment. For a second, it felt like it was not her house. She had mistaken that place for her own. She felt so distant from it. And yet, it also felt absolutely obvious that the lives they had should be their lives, that they should be the people they were. It all made sense now. The reason why it did was unreachable to Anne; yet she could feel it. It was all meant to be.

Anne opened the gate, crossed the yard and entered the house. She immediately sighed with relief, for she had not noticed how cold it was outside and it was nicely warm in the hall. She felt like a vagabond or a wild creature that had never set foot in a domestic, proper, clean environment. The moors had filled her with their immensity and she understood that she would need a moment to become human again.

Keeper and Flossy welcomed her return, running to her with their damp tongues out. It seemed to be a race and Keeper won. Anne stroked and embraced them. She laughed at their excitement, then ordered them to calm down.

She turned to the clock that looked so dark and threatening, but it was not that late. No one was in the dining room yet. She joined her sisters and Tabby in the kitchen to let them know she was back. The dogs followed her.

"There you are, love!"

Tabby had turned round at the vague sound of her footsteps and looked both relieved and mad.

"There I am."

"But you're quite drenched!"

Tabby almost ran to her and took Anne's cloak off her shoulders.

"Come to the fire, quick!"

It was a passionate order, the type none of them three would dare ignore, even as adults. Anne walked to the fireplace diligently and stood in front of it, quite used to obeying her grandmother-like servant.

"You'll all make me go mad, wandering on the moors at night with so little on your shoulders and so many dangers around! Do you want the death of me?"

Neither Anne, Charlotte, nor Emily replied. Tabby was not expecting any answer, only delivering her usual speech. The speech that she had first pronounced to Emily, who had always ignored it, but she knew Anne was too gentle to tell her frankly that she would probably return to the wild the following day.

Charlotte was folding the shirts that had been hanging to dry since the night before. She looked focused on her task and remained silent. Emily was mixing dough with energy, her face expressionless and her movements assertive.

"I hope you're freezing, missy," Tabby continued. "I really hope you are!"

Anne knew the old maid was worried about her and it was her way to keep it a secret, replacing fear with anger.

"I am a little cold, yes," Anne admitted.

She had approached her hands to the fire to warm them and noticed how red they were. How dry. Her fingertips were burning.

"Of course you are!"

Tabby seized a flap of her dress, touched her arms and shoulders with strength and exclaimed, "You're all wet! Go and get changed immediately!"

Anne took her writing and sketching supplies and went up to her room without a word.

She spread her humid dress on the chair to make it dry at best and put on the first thick and warm thing she could find.

She probably had some time before dinner… Perhaps she could allow herself a few more minutes to spend on her own.

She sat at her desk and closed her eyes to throw herself back to the moors, to where she had imagined it all, to the place that had made words emerge and fly in her head. After a moment, Anne opened her lids again, seized her pen and continued writing.

It felt both natural and distant to write such a story. She was constructing scenes so far, but she could clearly see where she was heading. How different it felt from the previous work! Had she changed that much? This novel – yes, she had decided, it would be a novel – was so different from *Agnes Grey*. So dangerously different… So deliciously as well.

She knew some scenes and characters would be painful to give birth to and describe, yet she had deliberately chosen to use the tip of her pen to open up her chest and relieve her heart.

Perhaps her novel would be read someday. *Agnes* had initially interested her sisters only but had been appreciated by experts too. Would she dare imagine this one would attract more eyes?

If it did, would the readers appreciate her work? What would they think of it? Anne remembered Charlotte's words after she had read Agnes's story and she refused to hear them again. No. She needed to evolve, develop her mind and see further and, above all things, she needed to grow up.

She was proud of her work for *Agnes*, but that new story – she could feel it – was of a different sort. Darker. Intense. No soothing comfort was to be offered. Anne was aiming at truth, authenticity; yet truth and authenticity were sometimes uneasy and distasteful. She would not simply amuse the reader [16]. She refused to limit her ambition to the give innocent pleasure[17]. It would be a story inside another story, for the errors and abuses of society[18] often hid like snakes in their holes.

Anne had changed. Yes, she had changed that much. She felt her mind and heart were enveloped in a new mist. Agnes's story had been the first chapter of her life; that novel would be the rest of it.

The door suddenly opened and Charlotte appeared.

"Anne, dinner's ready. We've been calling for you."

She did not wait for an answer and went back down. Anne had jumped, as though her sister had forced her out of a dream. She blinked and looked down at her writing book. She had written hastily, with an energy that had apparently threatened the pages to pierce them. Arrows, erasures and her right-slanted handwriting made her book look very untidy; yet it all appeared perfectly readable to Anne.

She would have to continue later, however. She stood up and left her room. On her way to the stairs, she noticed that Branwell's bedroom door was shut. Anne thought that he must have woken up and would be waiting for dinner

---

[16]Preface
[17]"
[18]"

downstairs. But when she came into the dining room, only Charlotte and her father were seated. Emily and Tabby were approaching with dishes in their hands and Anne took a seat quickly to free their way to the table.

None of them mentioned Branwell's absence. His presence in the house usually caused anxiety and tension in their muscles and those were often palpable; his absence fostered fear, uneasiness and misery.

Branwell had been able to play the role of the proper son and brother for five days. Five days. Anne wondered what five days meant to her brother, what they had felt like. While she and their family had lived their lives and completed their tasks quite peacefully, what had it been like for Branwell?

And what was it like for Charlotte? She had barely said a word during those five days and seemed absent. She had fought back, reached out in herself for the courage to self-defence and she had been strong and wise to do so, yet Anne suspected a little part of her sister had gone somewhere she could not fetch it. No words felt sufficient or soothing enough. Charlotte always disliked – feared – physical intimacy, did not know how to react to it and Anne's comforting arms felt useless. The purple marks Branwell had drawn on the sides of his sister's neck were hidden from their father's eyes by a white veil – a lie, a piece of fake purity used to conceal the traces of sin and rage – but it was only cloth, as delicate and thin as a veil was and Charlotte seemed to hide her entire being under it.

Her sister felt her eyes on her and Anne looked away, swallowing back a rush of powerlessness, compassion and worry.

She was not surprised not to share dinner with her brother. She had never trusted that quiet, abstinent period would last long and the picture of Branwell's dislocated-looking body and pale face was swinging in her head. Anne was too reasonable to believe that the scenes she had been writing all afternoon had had any fatal influence on her brother's weakness to yield to temptation; however, she did find it strange and unpleasant.

CHAPTER 8

As strange and unpleasant as it was, Anne nonetheless continued writing. She felt that new story pulsing in her veins. She remembered how much she had desired to write Agnes's story, how much she had wanted to tell the life of someone who would never get heard in reality; someone who was neither this nor that, neither high nor low. Someone who never truly knew where her place was and therefore could rely on herself only. She had been that someone and still was somehow. Anne had realised that she might have to be a governess again in the future, yet it was an idea that she found difficult to accept. She imagined herself surrounded by children – children who would not be her own, strong-headed and spoilt ones – in a dark room she would have to stay in most of the day, as a lonely creature, a bird in a cage.

Anne shivered. She made a silent prayer not to feel trapped again, ever, or alone.

Agnes's story had healed some invisible wounds she had felt. She hoped this one would soothe others. Deeper ones. Foul ones. That new story was not about children or the human and professional experience of a young girl discovering the world. It had to contain a profound aspect – secrets being revealed, dark truths being unveiled.

Anne had made some decisions. Names, towns and a plot were written down. She wrote and erased, thought and wrote again. Other times the words would fly in her head and it would be her mission to tiptoe and catch them, as though there were butterflies that needed to be chased and kept safe. Or, other times again, writing could be freeing – and easy. It was only a matter of opening the wound and letting the blood flow out. Sometimes the blood rushed. And it was made of words and images that had long needed release. Anne never felt closer to her real self than when those God-given moments occurred. Those moments were priceless, magical. Divine.

They had a darker side too, however, for God could give and the devil make pay. Anne had to pay back with minutes, sometimes hours, of pain and misery. Disturbing thoughts, disturbing pictures and bitter memories could invade her. Yet Anne always chose God's path and rejected the suffering, uprooting it from her mind like a bad weed from a garden.

Several weeks passed and were made of the same components. Anne followed a peaceful routine – a quiet line of prayers, chores, books and writing. The days were both too long and too short. They were all the same; one could have interchanged them had they been tangible. Anne was not bothered by such a thing. Knowing another same day would come was comforting and it was the promise she would be able to dive into her own head again very soon and continue writing.

She had met them – all of them – those characters. They were so similar to people she knew or had been acquainted with. When she read descriptions she would make of them, she could see them again and felt proud; for when she did, she knew the mission had been accomplished.

The description of her main female character was to be offered differently. It would lay on several pages, perhaps in the entire book, like a mystery to solve or a piece of needlework to complete. She deserved it. Anne sometimes closed her eyes and imagined her as she thought she herself was – or aspired to become. She did not want to portray another innocent, blind girl – her own mind had changed, she herself had evolved and she felt she needed to explore the new rooms in it. Yes, it was like a new house she had very recently purchased and had yet to visit its most mysterious nooks. Yet Anne knew such maturity had to be acquired through "age and experience" of life – and pain. Her character would have to have experienced life already.

There had to be an innocent protagonist, however. Someone who would lead, then accompany, the reader in their journey of discovery. Anne had thought about it and had decided that the character would be male. Oh, the thought of erecting surprise and even disapproval vaguely crossed her mind – and then settled far on a lonely island. Writing was a synonym for freedom and honesty, and Anne was allowed to give life to anyone and anything she judged right and true, however troublesome it might be for others.

An even more innocent character needed to be given birth to – her heroine's child. A boy putting into question the education that the little ones of his sex were given, representing hope and the possibility of a brighter future through a moral, proper upbringing and despite an irresponsible, repulsive parent, he was named after.

Anne knew ideas would come and go along the process of creation, but she could see what she was after. It was almost as though she could already see the lines written and read the book in her mind. The work was done; experiences had been lived, emotions felt, disillusion, acceptance had passed and the need for healing was knocking at the door. It was now time to give a conscious shape and a rightful morale to it.

It was about midnight when Anne formed that sentence in her mind, about midnight when she heard some noise from the yard. She ceased writing, paused, wondered if she was hearing footsteps on the grass of the yard and perhaps laughs; Anne was still unsure. She turned to Charlotte, who was sleeping soundly. She would be the only one able to hear anything, for her father must have been fast asleep, too. Emily's bedroom door was shut and Tabby's sleep had always been so heavy. Anne seized her pen again as silence had come. She must have imagined it all, she thought. She could be so concentrated, navigating in her personal sea of pictures and words…

No. This time she was sure she had heard something. Had Emily gone and fetched Branwell at the Black Bull already? She might not have heard her leave… But it was not that late; her sister was usually reading or writing at that time of night.

Branwell.

Anne, as well as the entire family, had stopped hoping her brother would join them for dinner and spend an early night at home. The five days he had tried to do so had been a lie, to them and to himself – Branwell was not able to be respectable or responsible anymore. The memory of his attitude towards Charlotte might have been too heavy a burden to bear – he needed to forget. It was a vicious cycle, Anne thought. A never-ending spiral of suffering. And it was so selfish, too. So cowardly. It was pain not properly handled.

Anne stood up at the third sound she heard and went down the stairs quietly, heading for the door. Keeper had remained alert at the top of the stairs; Flossy had woken up when she had left the room. Both dogs followed her faithfully and Anne felt relieved not to be alone in the dark hall. She hesitated and then unlocked the door and opened it, armed with all her courage in case someone or something terrible appeared.

It was so dark outside, so cold. The sky was starless and as black as a mourning veil; the wind was like bites on the flesh, freezing like death. And indeed, Anne's heart stopped when she looked down at the half-perceptible shadow lying at her feet – and when she recognised it.

Could it be Branwell's shadow? Was it really her brother sleeping and snoring on the threshold?

Anne clenched her jaw. She could not allow herself to be weak, or give way to shame, disgust and melancholy. Instead, she wondered what Emily would do. Pragmatic, strong Emily. She would not waste any more time thinking; she would act.

Anne knelt near her brother and called his name to wake him up. She first did it softly and gently, for she knew his temper when he was not himself and she feared a burst of unreasonable emotions. But Branwell kept snoring. Anne shook him. Nothing. Of course. Her brother's sleep was not a natural one. It was not fatigue after a day of toil blessed by peaceful rest. It was a sort of sleep that came from lack of self-respect and abandonment. It was the sort of sleep that aroused foul body odours the following day, the sort that did not cure dizziness and that awakened self-hatred, which could often be used as a weapon against others – the ones who stood close, the ones who cared the most.

Branwell had stolen the purity of sleep.

Anne stopped fearing her brother's reaction and shook him harder. Hit him. He finally woke and groaned. He opened his eyes; his lips were trembling and he did not seem to know where he was. His eyes were two empty light bowls. Even in the dark night, Anne could see them glistening.

Branwell had to blink three times to recognise her face he had yet known his entire life. Anne thought that perhaps she should leave him there. Perhaps he deserved to sleep in the cold immensity and wake up the next morning with a bag of shame in his heart. Perhaps that would teach him.

And then she remembered no such lesson could ever be taught, that her brother was not even willing to learn.

Anne stood up. She had felt her hands become icy cold and her body shiver. She felt dizzy herself, as if she had been the one drinking. A hundred pounds of emotions she could not yet name had crushed her brain and invaded her chest. Anne, however, obeyed her good nature and for the sake of their father and in the name of their past and ancestors in common, grabbed her brother, sighed and raged against him for being so heavy, struggled to awaken that body of his and help him remember how to sit and get up. Her back burnt, yet she did not give in.

Branwell pushed her away several times and Anne nearly lost her balance and fell. Nevertheless, each time, she went back into combat. She thought that they must look as if they were fighting, and perhaps they were a little; but Anne knew she had God and good sense on her side and so she eventually managed to make her brother stay still and get back on his feet. They were both shaking from the cold, but it somehow made her steady and even more determined in her self-given mission.

Branwell was giggling. Or trying to speak and trembling, she could not tell. He was staggering so immensely that Anne, on numerous occasions, almost fell with him.

She felt so light and so tiny. A ladybird fighting a storm.

They finally reached the threshold and entered the hall. Anne closed the front door with her foot and turned back round, looking at the stairs that had suddenly turned into an enemy she could not yet vanquish. They headed for the dining room instead. Anne shushed her brother, fearing he would wake their father and let go of him once they had got close enough to the sofa. Branwell landed on it like a heavy bag of corn and crashed, falling back into the unconscious hell he had left.

CHAPTER 9

Nights could be gentle and blow a timid wind with the sweetest memories of him. Or they could be furious and resentful, mad at an invisible might; during those nights, Anne's sleep was agitated.

It started peacefully at that time. He emerged in her unconscious mind softly and slowly, as if her brain were drawing him, trait after trait. When William Weightman's figure eventually appeared distinctively, Anne smiled in her sleep. He was smiling, too. He looked quite the same – his curls were delicate and there was that sparkle in his eyes. Anne sighed. How easy life could be! She could not remember why she would sometimes worry. Everything was so peaceful with that face near her.

An angel – or a monster – woke her. An angel who would have wanted to spare her even more pain when she would wake up, realise that none of it had been real and experience loss again. Or a monster that would have deprived her of the only things which would bring him back to her – dreams.

She woke gently, however, and her eyes looked so distant, so empty, reminding her of two small, white china cups when she got up and saw her reflection in the mirror. None of it had been real. It had all been a dream. He was definitively gone. To a land she prayed for to exist, above the skies, to a heavenly garden she refused to imagine was only an object of comfort to humans who feared death or who were not satisfied with their earthly lives.

William Weightman was no more. He was no more. Prayers, poems, dreams – none had brought him back. Sometimes she would imagine him resting on a quiet shore, surrounded by daisies and drowning in the sunlight; yet she also feared it was a childish way to imagine Paradise. She would never dare question the existence of Heaven out loud, certainly not to her father and not even to Emily, who had her own odd vision of it; but she wondered what it looked like, what it was like to be there – whether she should have taken what the Holy Book said for granted, if she should have read the description of Heaven from a journalistic, neutral point of view, or with the eye of a romantic poet hoping for perfect beauty.

Perhaps Branwell was right and Paradise appeared to them in dreams – fuzzy dreams inspired by excess. How come he was the lucky one who got to meet their mother and sisters in his sleep? Yet, even though their deaths had been excruciating and had draped their family in a thick shroud, the most recent loss had been a shock, depriving Anne of all hope that fills humans with blessed contentment, visions of a shared future and the tranquil, firm certainty that people you have created and shaped will outlive you. That recent loss was a stone – a rock, a black one – in her chest. She still expected to catch a glimpse of him when she walked to church sometimes and had to keep a straight face once she remembered such a simple, heart-racing little thing would never happen again.

Then she would confide in her writing book and find some comfort in the lines she would produce. She was bearing him inside her and gave life to poems he and her love for him would inspire.

Only ink and paper helped. And the wind, the moors. Sometimes the everyday chores and tasks. She could not confide in her sisters. Her emotions were too extreme to be shared and they would all have felt uneasy had she ever tried. Their brother occupied their thoughts too much anyway.

Their brother!

Anne had a quick wash and dressed promptly before running down the stairs to wake Branwell, who must still have been fast asleep on the sofa in the dining room. She had no idea what time it was exactly. Charlotte was still asleep, invisible and tiny under the thick and warm blanket, but the sun was up and she knew that her father, Emily and Tabby must have been, too.

No one. No one was in the dining room. Where had Branwell gone? Had he been able to wake in the middle of the night and go back to sleep in his bed? Anne doubted so. She climbed up the stairs nonetheless and checked her brother's bedroom. It was as messy and dirty as the last time she saw it, but Branwell was not in it. Had Emily seen him when she got up and lent him her own room? Yet, why would she do such a thing when his was available?

Anne shivered. Was Branwell downstairs being given a lecture by their father? Had they fought? Had her brother raised his voice? She had not heard anything in her sleep and the parsonage did not feel upside down – yet perhaps, the two men were having a conversation in their father's study and Branwell was expected to give an explanation.

The only way for Anne to make sure that everything was all right in there was to bring her father his morning tea. She ran down to the kitchen, checked Tabby's unperturbed expression and poured the tea into the cup herself. In her haste, Anne forgot to knock on the door and her father looked up in surprise.

"Anne," he said as a reaction to her unusual entrance.

"Father. I am sorry. Your tea."

She realised she was a little out of breath, but sighed with relief when she noticed that her father was alone – writing and reading at the same time, certainly studying, or transcribing some text. No flush of recent passionate, dramatic discussion was colouring his face.

Anne left the room, wondering where her brother was. Neither her father nor Tabby seemed to have seen him yet. The idea that Branwell woke up and went back to the Black Bull after she carried him into the house and helped him lie down on the sofa crossed her mind. If he had, where had he slept? Had he slept at all? Had he got lost, too drunk to find his way back home? Had he got himself into trouble again? Was he all right?

Worry was a bad weed that could grow so very fast and Anne knew her brother so well and had so little hope about him left, that her worry grew to become as high as a tree. She was the only one who had seen him the night before and she felt that it was her duty to find him.

Anne seized her cloak and entered the town. She ignored the staring faces, the cold on her hands and cheeks, her shaking jaw and the dangerously slippery cobbles still wet with night rain and winter morning dew.

Branwell was nowhere to be found. Anne refused to blacken her brother's name with a deeper disgrace[19] by spreading the rumour of another shameful night of Branwell Brontë, and did not ask anyone if they had seen him. It felt so difficult to do so anyway, for Anne's timidity and anxiety, if not agony, were wrestling too hard in her. She hurried back to the parsonage, fetched Flossy and headed for the moors as fast as she could. The faithful creature could feel she was allowed to run loose that day, jumped around Anne, ran back and forth, barking here and there. Perhaps she could feel her distress and it made her anxious too. Anne kept looking around her – for the familiar silhouette of her brother, for red hair popping out at a distance, for a jacket, a shoe, a cravat – on the grass, the hills and the freezing horizon.

The wind felt threatening that day. Anne realised how powerful, how menacingly powerful, the long-loved moors could be and for the first time, feared them. And she knew she would hate them if they kept her brother hidden from her – if they had harmed him in any way.

Anne screamed. She screamed his name, screamed at the god-like wind that seemed to punish her for whatever wrong deed she might have done. Flossy turned to her mistress, alert, and began barking again. Louder and louder. Anne could feel some tears – tears of rage, she decided – tickle her cheeks.

---

[19] *The Tenant*

"Flossy..." she whispered, as if begging for help.

Suddenly, she heard someone call her own name. She knew that voice—it was not the wind's.

Anne turned round and gasped at the sight of Branwell. It was really him. He was there and he looked all right. As all right as Branwell could be. When he got closer, Anne noticed how pale, how ill, how skinny and how terrible he looked. The wind did her a favour by covering her brother's odour and breath, so she could only imagine what he smelt like.

Witnessing his state, one more time, and remembering the stench that usually accompanied such pallor, such glassy eyes and such self-hatred combined with indecent nonchalance, mockery and the underlying threat that appearance could burst into flames and transform itself into a monster in fire, spitting unwanted words and showing physical brutality – witnessing and remembering all of that, Anne felt her worry being replaced with a rage she had no recollection of having ever felt. Where had he been? Why could he not behave properly, normally, responsibly? Why did he believe that he was the only one who was in pain? And why – why had he had to show such violence? Why did he grasp their sister's neck, shake her like a doll and push her to the wall?

A sour taste invaded Anne's mouth and words that usually respected her lips as a non-violent fortress were threatening to slip out that time.

And Anne let them out.

It was not a disgusted reprimand Charlotte would give, a disappointed look followed by ignorance their father would not control, or an expression of worry and powerlessness Tabby would endure; it was a cry. A speech that Anne had no power or will to interrupt, not even to catch her breath. A speech that had a heartbeat as fast and strong as a thoroughbred horse's. A bleeding speech, with each word was a drop of blood that flew out of Anne's invisible wounds and that left Branwell's cheeks.

Anne described the night before to him – Branwell did not remember any of it. She repeated the rude words he often had for his sisters, who were ruining their mental health for his sake. She mimicked his attitude after a night at the pub and accused him of being a dark cloud above their heads.

But Anne mostly allowed her secrets to flow out. And her secrets were made of how she felt around him, about him, how his words and behaviour worried, frightened and exhausted her. How scared she was when she noticed how thin Emily looked, how old their father was, how hurt and shaky Charlotte.

She did not cry; her voice was firm; her mind was clear and her eyes were wide open. Branwell's ghost-like face did not move or shake her. Nor did his mumbling, pathetic apologies and promises. They were, for the first time in a long time, for the first time in years, for the first time since adulthood had reached and caught them, facing each other with honesty. Anne's words were blades cutting her brother's flesh here and there. The veil above their heads, that veil weaved in fear of disappointment, loss, disapproval and loneliness in the world, was pierced. Anne had pierced it with words as sharp as thorns and was digging into the hole she had made a little deeper. For she could not stop. Her words were like ocean waves, too, and she was a weak seaweed, crushed by them and dancing under their weight.

Anne could feel her power, her power over her brother. Over another human soul. She could feel the power of words, of honesty, of hurtful truth – and she felt like a queen. Yet, although Anne was first surprised by that rush of power, although she dizzily felt drawn to it for a minute, she soon tasted the bitterness of it and, since thirst for power was not lying in her nature, Anne remained true and self-controlled. She did not accuse her brother wrongly or deliver falsities. Her words were being released by rage but also a feeling of not being able to endure anymore; and Anne governed it all. Letting those words out felt like grasping a tumour out of her chest. Or brain. Or stomach.

Branwell could see it did and had the decency not to interrupt or contradict his sister. He knew her voice had been shut down for long, buried and left behind. He could hear her despair hidden under the descriptions that she gave of his looks and attitudes, her fear of losing him, her exhausting wish to keep their family as a whole; her pleading for change, perhaps, her disgust and hate, too. Branwell was sorry, but his shame and self-hatred were such that he could not allow them loose within him. Clearing the way to them, permitting them to rule, would have annihilated him.

His sister's truth was burning him. He had clenched his jaw, his fists and focused on how to turn those inflamed arrows into raindrops rolling down his skin. But knowing

Anne was only being sincere, not cruel, was worse. And many arrows hit his heart.

Finally, Anne was done. She had said it all. Now that the veil was pierced, that the words were out and flying in the air between them, what was left? Anne did not know if she had hope for her brother to heal after that scene. It was all so blurry. She felt relieved, empty and as though she was not even expecting anything in particular. She had said what she had to say and that was that. It was all that mattered for now.

As for Branwell, he knew he had to say something. He could not perceive whether he was telling the truth or lying when he promised his sister he was quitting drinking. In fact, and she had to believe him, he had been wandering in the moors, absorbing their wisdom, thinking and deciding so. He swore and promised again.

Was he telling her the truth? Only Anne knew. And so, she repeated herself.

"I do not believe you are renouncing that poison, Branwell. You keep breaking your resolutions. And the demon of drink is as black as the demon of opium and as hard to get rid of[20] – for yes, brother, I know about that bottle of laudanum that you keep secret. I can see my words upset you, but they did for an instant only and the emotion won't last. And when it's gone, you will not be able to keep your word. Your promises are like the air and they transcend you. And it's not even your fault. I can see you are telling me what you think I need to hear, but you

---

[20] *The Tenant*

are mistaken. I am not hoping for anything, nor am I expecting any glorious decision from you. I am full, full of you and your disease. You are everywhere, all the time, in my head, in my heart, in my nightmares, in every line of worry on our father's and sisters' faces. I am tired of wondering if you will be yourself tonight, or if I or Emily will have to take care of what is left of our brother. I am tired of never knowing what to expect, how to feel, what to plan, or what to hope for. I am tired of that disappointment and even pain when a pleasant day or evening gets interrupted by your degrading conduct. I am tired of fearing for you, your safety, your wellbeing, your happiness, your health; or if you will put us all into financial difficulties, betray us or physically hurt another one of us. I am tired of you, brother. Of what you have become. You promise me you will never drink again, will behave properly, as a gentleman. But I think the gentleman in you has drowned in all the liquor you gulped – and is gone. My brother is gone. Because you have been drinking for so long, started so young. You do not know what behaving as a gentleman means. The brilliant man you should have become is gone. He is no more. He is no more. Definitively gone. Just like so many other things and just like us inside. For I do feel changed and different now. God and the moors be my witnesses."

It looked like Branwell's soul was wrestling to get out of his body. He looked confused, lost, incapable. He looked like a child who needed to be taken care of. He looked as though he was crushed by a weight he could not raise, a mountain he was buried alive under. Branwell Brontë was struggling to be Branwell Brontë again.

Anne mourned her brother. She had been in mourning for so long now, for ever since she could remember. She had woken with grief in her heart that morning and at the back of her head and even her eyes and she was now grieving again.

The world had been reduced to an island, a minuscule kingdom Anne was the monarch of. Only the both of them and the whistling, slapping wind and the frozen grass and earth under their feet and those emotions that came as a pack, a heavy pack, in which none could distinguish itself from another, lived in that kingdom. After a while, Anne perceived something, such as disbelief and guilt, that she kept at the threshold of their tiny universe. They were not welcomed, not today. She also met with pride and allowed that one in. For it had an unknown smell Anne wanted to inhale deeply, perhaps even taste freely. She closed her eyes and focused on it.

She could no longer feel her brother's presence, the cold, the humid air, her short breath, her choking-like corset and prison-like petticoats. She could no longer hear Flossy barking, Branwell's useless apologies and unconscious lies. She no longer cared what time it was, about reassuring Tabby she was well, about being home on time, about obeying, about duty, propriety, rules and society. She was no longer a daughter, only the youngest sister. She was a woman, an individual.

It was a blessed moment. Anne relished the minute it lasted and prayed for some sparkles of it to stay in her forever.

What a dramatic scene! Anne thought when she opened her eyes again. They were standing on a northern hill, like two moor crows facing each other, the insolent wind waltzing with her hair and roaring at his face, as though to support and underline Anne's words. Branwell looked like a shipwrecked mariner cleaving to a raft, blinded, deafened, bewildered[21]. It seemed that he felt the waves sweep over him and, as always, saw no prospect of escape[22].

He could feel the wind's ferocity, for he said, "Others have tried to save me, Annie. And none succeeded. I'm a lost cause. I've lost friends I scared off, ruined, mocked and exhausted. And you're right, I've lost myself, too. I just don't want to lose you, any of you… *Ah!* I want to scream!"

Anne felt for her brother, although remained tranquil and distant. Her heart could not be reached that easily now. She took a step ahead and held him in her arms for a minute or two. Thin, red-haired creatures holding in the wild. They belonged to it, for that instant. They were one on the moor.

---

[21] *The Tenant*
[22] "

CHAPTER 10

Anne would not head back to the parsonage. She would not feel trapped again. Instead, she sent Flossy back with Branwell and waited for them to be out of sight to give in, lie down and let exhaustion invade her entire body.

Anne slept for the most part of the day. She rose a different person, wondering what was right and what was wrong. Should she have delivered such honesty to Branwell earlier? Could he have understood it then? Or had it been the right time for both of them? Should she have kept it all for herself? Had she made a mistake, only hurt him and ruined their relationship? Would he feel so bad that he would simply drown his sorrows in pints? Or had she, on the contrary, saved them both? Plus, for how long exactly had she needed to tell her brother all these things? Why had she not done it sooner? What had prevented her from doing so? Cowardice? Shyness? Was shyness a form of cowardice? Was it simply the Christian fear of hurting her brother? Was it only that? Was it not hypocritical to believe such a thing?

Had she enjoyed it, telling him the truth? Had she enjoyed hurting him a little? Hitting one limb after the other with her words? Anne feared His opinion on the matter and yet she feared being judged as a hypocrite by Him even more. And so, she had to be honest one more time – she had. It had been rejoicing, just a little, to hurt the person who kept hurting her and the ones she cared for the most. It had felt only fair.

Anne begged for God's forgiveness although she also accepted the fact that she was no saint. And she had shown no cruelty, after all. She had only revealed the truth, her truth. She had meant well, covering it with generosity and empathy and care, but it had not helped her brother or her family. It had not helped her. It had not helped anyone or made things easier. Anne understood that generosity, empathy and care could take various forms, sometimes the most unexpected shapes. Her honesty had burnt him. She had seen it. Yet the cure to the disease was hiding in the same place as the disease itself: in Branwell's mind. And only his mind could decide to put an end to that bad dream they were all stuck in – to try and try again and again.

The fall had felt so brutal, yet it had not been. Branwell had been a promising little boy, the only one among so many sisters. He had been talented, creative, vigorous, lively and witty. He had written so much, spent so much time with them, shared so much with the three of them. Imagination, childhood, loss. Anne missed her brother; she missed the little boy. He had discovered the world, faced disillusion, reality and rejection. He had slowly turned into the most monstrous and yet also the most sensitive being Anne could think of. His sensitivity had turned him into a monster. Branwell had not been able to bear the real world. They had been protected from it, high on their northern hill facing the wild, sheltered from its polluting rumours, black smoke and noise. London had been too much to bear. Branwell had not been the same since London.

Yet Anne kept searching in their past for some explanation for that transformation. If their mother had been alive, would he have—

Or perhaps, it was the loss of Maria, of Elizabeth.

Or perhaps, their father's strict upbringing. Anne had to be honest again and admit to herself that their father had used rigidity in their education as a promise of future success. He had also used it as a shield, Anne was sure of it, against pain. Loneliness. The weight of duty, the weight of six little children to provide for, the weight of God. Perhaps, Anne wondered, rigidity had not cooperated so well with Branwell's nature. Perhaps, it had been like fire on a wet bush; perhaps, it had made sparkles in her brother's frame that none of them had suspected.

Perhaps that was where his anger came from. Perhaps he resented them, him, for shutting his spirit down.

Could he find liberty in sin now, then? Could drinking and gambling excessively release something that had failed to grow naturally and express itself with calm? Had that woman in Thorp Green helped him release that freedom, too? Had she been an addiction that her brother had not even been conscious of? Was she still?

When Anne got up and headed back to the parsonage, she could feel how light her head and chest were. She had crossed a border and entered a new land, a place she had never been before. She could feel that she was standing at the edge of herself, where all emotions meet, making one and a whole of who one is. She had never felt so close to her real being. Her real being was the new land.

How foreign she was! How foreign to her own person! She was so profound, unexpectedly different from who she had once thought she was. The path to self-discovery was laying in front of her; it was not so invisible in her eyes.

A lightning strike broke the purple sky into two, yet Anne did not fasten her pace. Even nature would not rule over her this time.

The world groaned again. Anne had arrived home and shut the door behind her. No Branwell was to be seen. Anne did not look for him. Was this what having had too much to drink felt like? That liberation, like a cloud of easiness, confidence, nonchalance – Anne could understand how one could lose sight of how many sips of it they had had and wanted more, evermore, of its tasty consequences. Yet she remained quiet, did not seek company or foolishness. Anne went up to her room and wrote.

She had, in a way, been married to Branwell. So had Emily, so had Charlotte. And they all had acted differently, as different wives would have. None of them was attached to him through a golden ring placed by a promise to God, but the same blood was running in their veins. The same boiling, dancing nerves that cried for the same need for stories and altered universes. The same eyes on life; the same hearts, perhaps.

Branwell was the husband she had not asked for, a sibling she did not comprehend. She was linked to him by a pact she had never signed. There was no way out.

Branwell would always be Branwell. And her character would always be what he was. Cursed. By his own decisions.

Anne would fill Arthur Huntingdon's pathway with lessons and opportunities for good behaviour sent by Providence. Yet man is the master of his own choices. Anne now also believed that witnesses were offered free will, too. And though some choices first appeared as disturbing possibilities, they were, in fact, silent gifts from heaven to earth.

Free will. And self-protection. Helen Huntingdon would be offered one of those gifts and the chance to start over. A fresh start. Yes, fresh and clean. Pure. As pure as the child she would be given.

Anne wrote and time flew. It was like a secret they shared, an agreement between them – she would write and the hours would be minutes.

Anne was almighty. She gave Helen Huntingdon the reason and courage she knew would be her saviours. She painted her husband as a fiend, even when it was not truly what she had first meant to do. The choices he would make, she knew them. She knew where they came from and why he would make them. She knew even when he did not. They were the choices Branwell would often make.

Anne realised that her brother was not as unpredictable as she had thought. He was not free. Nor was Arthur Huntingdon. Their decisions were dictated by primary needs – primary illusions. They were chained to poisons – imprisoned, tormentedly married to them. Anne was not the caged wife, nor were Emily or Charlotte. They were free – for their minds were not intertwined with restless desire for the deadly cure.

Arthur Huntingdon would be a fiend to attempt to darken his wife's pure soul, to murder her young hopes and to break her loving heart; yet he would also be a life lesson. A cruel one, a difficult one to face. But one impossible to forget.

Anne looked up from her notebook when a distinct smell approached her nose. She knew it was late – she had to go downstairs and write in the dining room not to disturb Charlotte's sleep. So surely Tabby could not be cooking and the smell could not be the smell of food.

And yet something was undoubtedly burning. Anne's heart jumped in her chest. If no one was cooking in the kitchen, what was burning?

She quickly checked the fireplace behind her; all was right. She ran to her father's study and checked all the chimneys downstairs. Nothing. When she ran back to the hallway, a vague cloud of smoke was polluting the air in the staircase.

"Lord help us!"

Anne seized the bottom of her skirts and climbed the stairs in haste. The smoke had found a way to get out of Branwell's bedroom, slithering out of it from the bottom of the door.

Anne froze. Fire…

The word remained stuck in her throat. Fire in the house. Fire in her brother's bedroom.

Branwell was on fire. He was burning... He was in hell already and surrounded by flames... There was nothing to be done. He could not be saved.

When Anne remembered how to breathe, think properly and move, her desperate knocks on Branwell's door obtained no response. She called for him – very loud, it seemed, yet perhaps not enough. Anne could not tell.

A rush of black wind pushed her aside. It felt like a storm or an unearthly power and Emily appeared in Anne's sight. She did not say a word. Her eyes were gigantic and she forced her way into their brother's room.

Anne was the spectator of the scene; it looked like a terrible passage from a novel. She had a vision and saw Emily carrying her brother out of the room. She was struggling. He looked so pale – different already. Asleep, extinguished. As white and yellowish as a candle, but not a lit one. A weight. He was their weight. Emily had saved their burden. She had brought him back from hell. She groaned and let his heavy body onto the passageway. He was drooling. His shirt was ripped and a thick, unpleasant smell emanated from him. A weight of flesh. A slug.

"Water, Anne!"

Wateranne. Water Anne. Water! Anne blinked and pushed her lying brother out of the way with all her might to get to the stairs and fetch a bucket. Charlotte was following her – Anne had not realised she was up. When they reached back into their brother's room, Anne found that her sisters' long, white nightgowns made them look like two angels trapped by flames and fighting mercilessly. Anne tried not to think of them arguing desperately against a decision that had already been made by God – though it did seem that they were fighting a battle that they had already lost.

They used water and blankets to extinguish the fire. Branwell had dropped the candlestick, which had started attacking the rug and sheets. Ashes of paper were flying all around them.

It was snowing cinder. Like a bad omen.

Some books had yet survived, Anne noticed. Some bottles, too.

Their father's face was blank. Standing on the threshold of Branwell's room, unwilling, or perhaps worried, to enter that nightmare, he remained silent.

The fire died. The silence that followed was somehow deafening and punctuated by Branwell's sobs and mumbles. The weight had come back to life. The slug had awakened.

Branwell spent the rest of the night and the nights that followed in their father's bed. The man he would claim to despise and often disrespected had become his companion in unconsciousness. Emily had offered him her own bed – she could not care less where she slept. Charlotte had not suggested anything. As for Anne, she had made a choice. Reality was helpless. Fiction was the answer. By spring, the novel was finished.

CHAPTER 11

Anne had drained herself, emptied and purified her mind and heart by writing and publishing a story that felt so close to home and it felt right. The book made more sense than what was happening on the first floor of the parsonage. Her imagination had been the only escape, the only way out, the only brush of fresh air that year. It had always been so, if Anne had to be honest; but when Branwell started coughing and filling the air with a foul smell and worry, imagination became oxygen.

Oxygen. It seemed like Branwell could not find any whenever he attempted to breathe. He had spent his entire adult life searching for air, for freedom, and they were now burning his throat. It sounded like it, at least. It sounded so painful to stay alive.

Was he being punished?

It was sunny, warm and peaceful, when Branwell coughed so hard that Emily had to lift up his head and help him sit up, so he would not choke on his own saliva. It was sunny and warm, yet Anne shivered. It felt like a giant's icy hand had seized and squeezed her heart when thick, dark drops came out of Branwell's mouth. They coloured his lips, which had become pale, and they coloured Emily's handkerchief with red dots that none of them wanted to see. They both knew what those dots meant. Everyone knew what they usually led to.

Each time the three sisters and Tabby took the dotted sheets away and replaced them with immaculate ones, it almost seemed like hope was possible. When they were interrupted in their daily chores or disrupted in their sleep by the sounds of painful coughs from the two men's room, hope became a distant memory and the sight of brownish stains on the fresh linen darkened their reality.

The doctor was called in, of course, and after a moment with Branwell, made an announcement all of them had expected. Anne had kept silent and still throughout the examination, waiting patiently on the landing for a diagnosis she already knew. Her father had turned into a statue in his study. Emily had kept invisible, locked in her room with Keeper and ink, two emotional guardians. Tabby had welcomed the doctor and gone back to her tasks, her emotions deeply shut in her chest, while Charlotte, only Charlotte, had found the strength and presence of mind to lead the gentleman to Branwell. She had stayed with the two of them in her father's bedroom, feeling like a nurse again and wondering if it was the lot of women to be the carers of men.

Her eyes remained fixed on her brother for once, knowing she could not waste another opportunity to look at him and feeling each bloody cough he let out in her own throat and lungs.

Branwell.

The doctor left. He did not do so taking all hope with him, as men of his profession often did, for, again, they simply had none. The illness had reached the core of Branwell's chest. They could ease his pains, but it was no surprise when September came with darker clouds and fewer wishes. And it painted their world grey. Their faces were five pearls with greyish eyes and dark expressions – soon their clothes would be dark, too.

The three of them had accomplished things, reached their goals and created universes. Yet it all was tasteless and Anne, who had always lived in her head, was now easily distracted from her imagination. She was not sure she would have wanted to escape anyway. For the first time in a long time, living reality was priceless.

Reality was Branwell still. That had not changed. Only Branwell's stormy rage, outbursts and wanderings had been replaced with sounds of physical agony and shared anguish. Anguish and expectation. Or an expectation made of anguish. Their father grew a few more lines on his forehead those days and he looked human and tired only when his son woke him in the middle of the night with loud coughs, red drops and violent shudders.

Anne had not told anyone, but she realised the anguish that she felt – that they all felt – was not new. It had grown silent in their chests for some years and Branwell had brushed the edge so many times that Anne suspected they were prepared.

He could not be saved.

That time, nothing would be better after a few hours or the next day. Anne had become used to the ups and downs that excesses implied. She had become used to liquid mistakes, hopelessness and bearing a brother that none of them, not even God or himself, could save. At that time, every day was a "down" day. No pause, no improvement, was promised in the end.

Only an infinite pause could be expected. An endless end.

When it came, breaking into the men's bedroom on a rainy day, Anne realised the mistake she had made. She was not prepared to lose her brother. There was no way to prepare for that. Perhaps God had relieved him of his sufferings – and perhaps also theirs – but Anne's reason grew rebellious. Dying at the age of thirty-one was no relief. It was a crime. God had committed a crime.

Where was her brother now? Was his soul drifting, flying all around her in the house—

Branwell. Was he there?

Anne remembered the mask their father had brought them one day when they were children. That mysterious mask. She was only four then – it was an eternity ago. And yet she remembered how freeing it felt to wear it, hide her expression and eyes and be allowed to say whatever she felt the need to say without being reprimanded for it. It had been as though Branwell had never stopped wearing it, as though he had forgotten it was still on his face.

What about that mask now? Was he hiding behind it, which somehow made him invisible to human eyes?

Anne opened her mouth, though no sound escaped from it. The air in her lungs was stuck. Some sort of swelling seemed to have formed at the bottom of her throat and stopped her from breathing properly, from speaking, from screaming.

B   R   A   N   W   E   L   L.

Her brother. Brother. Had she abandoned him? Bran. Her life and childhood companion. Her blood. The extension of her being. The continuity of her soul. Her brother.

Anne flinched in front of their father's bedroom door. Her sisters were in the room already. Anne could hear their busy footsteps on the wooden floor. They resonated in her head.

Oxygen. Oxygen.

She caught some air here and there and endeavoured to calm down.

She had to participate. She had to. Her sisters were suffering from the same pain as she and she could not allow herself to be tragic that day. Tears would have to wait until nighttime.

She came into the bedroom. Branwell was lying in the bed, surrounded with white. An angel. The picture was almost dazzling. White sheets, white shirt, white... body. God knew he had been no angel. Was He trying to comfort them? Branwell's red hair was the only vivid tint in this painting and that bright colour looked like a dare he would play on his creator. "I am no angel," he seemed to say. "Free me from all these immaculate pieces of fabric. I want no hypocrisy on my end. See my hair, as red as my rage and misery were in my life on Earth. As rebellious. *This* is me."

"Anne," Charlotte called.

Anne blinked and seized the bucket her sister was handing her. Now was not a proper time to daydream. She had to prove herself useful, helpful and, as always, choose courage over despair.

The water in the bucket was freezing. First, she worried about it before she remembered it did not matter anymore. Emily handed her a cloth and Anne drowned it in the bucket. Charlotte unbuttoned Branwell's shirt and took it off his shoulders. His chest had a purple tint in the morning light. Anne looked away and kept her eyes on their brother's spectacles, useless now and lying on their father's bedside table. When Emily lifted up Branwell's body to help Charlotte slip the shirt off of under him, Anne turned to them and it was only then that she truly felt his loss. Her sisters looked like two death fairies, two black angels, straight and grave as always. Grief drew certain lines on faces and theirs were marked profoundly.

They had lost a limb. Litres of blood. Pounds of life. Childhood and common memories.

Once more, Anne could not find enough air around her to fill her lungs. Yet she followed her sisters' example and remained silent.

It felt like they shared something more than blood now – an emotion, a state of being: the loss of a brother. Mourning. Invisible threads bound them together. A common past, a common experience, common pain and relief. They were sisters more than ever. Nothing could untie their hands now; no one would understand them better than they would understand each other. Even in silence. They were both doomed and blessed to remain together forever.

Anne knew the two siblings she had left by heart. She knew they both felt and thought the same way.

Charlotte looked tinier than ever. Her head was large, and her eyes hid their torment behind small, round spectacles. She was pale, tired and her cheekbones were so prominent that the circles under her eyes seemed to dig deeper into her skin. Her childlike hands summarised her better than any description Anne could ever have given of her sister. They were minuscule, weak and shaking; yet a stronger force seemed to control them and the trembling was perceptible only by those who would pay definite attention to this petite, silent, secretive woman.

Emily was a ghost. Her skin was transparent, her veins underneath nearly visible and no pinkish tint coloured her face. Her arms were thin, her chest flat, and there was a spectral beauty about her that she seemed to carry around. Like an aura as obvious and subtle as a flower fragrance. Emily seemed to dedicate all the energy she had left in her to becoming invisible. She was untouchable, unreachable. Keeper followed her to the moor, as quiet and solemn as his mistress, and pages and pages were certainly being covered in black ink; but Anne felt as though her sister had reached a place beyond a lonely island. Yet she felt closer to her than she had ever done.

CHAPTER 12

A funeral was organised rapidly. They were burying someone who had been condemned to an early death. He had rejoiced and tormented them and now he was no more.

Another hole had formed in Anne's chest, a hole Branwell had filled his entire life. Branwell's spot in her heart. His absence left a mark. A mark which felt so distinct that Anne almost wondered at not catching a glimpse of her brother somewhere around her. Branwell was absent at his own funeral. How dared he? How even stranger of her to be puzzled by such a thing... Anne felt so confused...

How slowly they were walking. How strongly separated from her own body she felt. She was following the horde automatically. Her legs and feet were obeying some mute order from the little mob and Anne thought that they all looked as though they were walking to their last and eternal residences – keenly and in silence – that they were all waiting in line for it. How odd.

She could see as she was walking the grave faces around her. She understood that people were showing respect to their loss – to a young soul which had flown away too soon. Too soon. Were they wearing masks, too? What would she tell them if she was wearing that mask?

Or were they hiding their thoughts from them – repeating to themselves that they had always known it would end that way? That young man, after all, had led a wild life indeed. They all knew about it. He had provoked fate, confronted God and now he was gone. As should be. No surprise, no, no surprise indeed.

Or perhaps, they were counting all the deaths that their family had endured. Perhaps they were wondering what was wrong with them – in that high, remote house in which they hid. Perhaps they were wondering who would be next. Or if their reverend was cursed.

Anne bit her lip when she realised how wrong her thoughts were. Their poor friends and inhabitants of Haworth were simply there to support their pastor and his family, and say farewell to a man they had known as a little boy.

Was there a curse, though? Were they cursed? Who would be next?

They eventually stopped walking. The churchyard was right in front of their house and yet it had felt such a tremendous journey.

Finally, that hole – that gap… Someone had dug a hole in the earth and Anne suspected it was for her to lie in it. Her heart was in there already. At the bottom of it. It was a gigantic piece of flesh covered in dirt.

She had lost two sisters as a child. It had been a tragedy and she had been sorry; but how different it felt to lose a sibling as an adult and with whom she had seen and experienced life, shared and felt the same things.

Anne had asked for "age and experience" as a child, wearing that mask. Branwell had brought it all to her, had been God's tool to teach her love, hope and hopelessness – which often led to resilience. She had gained "age and experience" through Branwell. He had shaped the beating part of her life – and now would lie underground.

No. That hole was not for her. They brought Branwell's coffin and they all played their roles in that ceremony of farewells to a wooden box. *God. My brother is dead.*

Few words were exchanged, pronounced. Loss, sometimes, is a stranger to words.

It was so cold. The rain was pouring; it felt as though they were standing in a furious river in the middle of winter. God was pitiless.

Anne wondered if it was raining to help them wash away their pain and remorse. Their relief. Their shame at being relieved. Washed away. Shoo. Off with you.

Branwell was gone. Gone with no sense, no meaning – gone at thirty-one. Gone.

They left the churchyard they had known forever and where dozens of neighbours, friends and relatives lay. Branwell was one of them now.

Anne, walking silently behind her sister, thought she might see his tombstone from Emily's bedroom window. She might try to later. Branwell was gone, but not so far, perhaps.

The rain kept pouring, offering them no rest and plunging them into a grey, muddy world that did not help with wanting to survive another day. Another grief.

And Emily was shivering. Her long and slender silhouette did not even seem to touch the earth. A spectre.

Anne should have known – Emily had never belonged to them. And when she shivered more severely, started coughing and growing whiter than she had ever been, Anne sought God's mercy with all the strength she had left.

She had wanted "age and experience." Yet when she recognised the dark spots that had dotted Branwell's sheets and shirts on Emily's handkerchief, Anne ceased seeking for them and she was glad that she had completed her novel, published it and shook a narrow, insular world with it. For watching the souls that peopled her fortress-like little universe leave forever was not a life Anne wanted to lead. She felt tired suddenly, which was unfortunate, for a thousand projects and dreams were, despite it all, dancing in her mind when she gave in to slumber.

THE END